READER PRAISE FOR THE ESSIEN SERIES

"A real page turner"

"Love the Essien family"

"My new favourite author"

"Excellent"

"Great series"

"Fantastic"

"I want to be like Felix Essien when I grow up!"

Kiru Taye

ALSO BY KIRU TAYE

The Essien Series
Keeping Secrets
Making Scandal
Riding Rebel
Kola
A Very Essien Christmas
Freddie Entangled
Freddie Untangled

Bound Series
Bound to Fate
Bound to Ransom
Bound to Passion
Bound to Favor
Bound to Liberty

The Challenge Series
Valentine
Engaged
Worthy
Captive

Passion Shields Series
Scars
Secrets
Scores

Men of Valor Series
His Treasure
His Strength
His Princess

Others
Haunted
Outcast
Sacrifice
Black Soul

Kiru Taye

First Published in Great Britain in 2019 by
LOVE AFRICA PRESS
103 Reaver House, 12 East Street, Epsom KT17 1HX
www.loveafricapress.com

5

DEDICATION

To those who fight so that we can live and love freely.

"All is fair in love and war."

~ John Lyly's *Euphues*

PART ONE

FAIR PLAY

CHAPTER ONE

LONDON, UNITED KINGDOM
OCTOBER 2007

IT IS SAID that a girl's first love is her father.

For nineteen-year-old Isha Saene, the First Princess of the Kingdom of Bagumi, this wasn't entirely true.

Not that she didn't adore her father or wasn't fond of him to an extent.

However, seeking affection from a man with two wives, eight children, and ninety-eight thousand citizens to govern had grown into a lost cause.

Getting a private audience with her father had become a rarity since she'd entered her teen years. As a pre-pubescent child, she had enjoyed spending time with him as he'd read her school reports and had beamed with pride and joy at the levels of distinction achieved in her academic studies. These days, no awards of merit or excellence from her schools got him to spend one-to-one time with her. He had other priorities.

Consequently, she had given up on vying for parental attention.

She desired a man of her own—someone who would devote time to her whether she was good, bad, or indifferent.

Hence, the reason she arrived early for class. She needed a good seat, which meant being one of the firsts to come in.

For other classes, she would sit mid-row. For this one, she chose the front row middle column, which gave her a direct view of the lecturer and the clean whiteboard.

Squeaks from the opening door announced the arrivals of other students. Most of the undergraduates in the law faculty made an effort with their appearances since it was Monday morning. But others looked like they hadn't recovered from their weekend of partying, bringing with them the smell of beer, smoke, and sweat.

Her phone buzzed, and she pulled it from the brown leather tote. The ID on the notification was for her second oldest brother.

His Royal Highness, Prince Azikiwe Saene—or plain old Zik as he was fondly named by family and friends—was the closest of her siblings. Compared to their rigid and conservative first brother, Crown Prince Zawadi, Zik was a fun-loving animal who didn't mind bending the rules once in a while. Although they'd had their share of squabbles, she seemed to be on the same wavelength with him most times. And he'd always been her champion and sometimes confidante.

Zik was a Formula One motor racing enthusiast and had gone to São Paulo, Brazil for a long weekend to watch the last Grand Prix of the season. When she hadn't heard from him by the time she'd left home this morning, she'd sent him an electronic note.

Now, she clicked on the icon and read his response: *'I got your message. Flew into London this morning.'*

'Welcome back. How was it?' she typed.

She didn't share his enthusiasm for long-haul flights across the Earth just to spend a couple of days watching men drive cars at break-neck speeds around the tracks. However, she enjoyed the stories about his adventures.

Her phone buzzed again. *'A thrilling weekend. I know you've got lectures so we'll talk after I've slept off this jet lag. Later.'*

Lucky for him, the Master's Degree he studied meant he didn't have lectures every day so he could afford to spend the afternoon in bed.

'Okay. Later. Xoxo.' She sent the last text and switched off her phone before storing it in her bag.

Her limbs were weighted as she thought about home. As a child nurtured within a large family, she could never complain of being lonely. However, privacy proved elusive.

With actions, words, and persons monitored by governesses, tutors, minders, and bodyguards, Isha had struggled to suppress her independent spirit and conform to protocols. The large entourage also worked as buffers between her and her parents. The constraints had weighed on her like heavy balls and chains around her neck.

Being the prime princess meant leading by example—modelling the perfection expected from the female members of the royal household.

She'd bid her time, and had waited for the right opportunity to spread her wings.

On her sixteenth birthday, when her peers had been throwing lavish, over-the-top sweet sixteen parties, she'd asked for one thing, knowing her father would have to grant her wish.

"Papa, when I go to study at university, I don't want to be Isha Saene."

First, King Ibrahim had laughed, assuming she'd cracked a joke. Then, he had raged, for months, at her audacious request. Finally, he'd caved in, after been persuaded by every member of the family she could recruit to her cause.

So here, she was Ruby Bagumi, an overseas student from a middle-class family. Her maternal grandmother Mina Fumi had given her the middle name of Ruby, and Bagumi was a generic surname just like Smith or Clark or Jones.

In this lecture hall, no one knew her identity. She had autonomy over her life and the liberty to be her true self. There was no adherence to strict protocols or etiquette—the most significant freedom of all.

The creaking door made her look up. Her heart jolted.

Professor Bassong entered the auditorium, the highlight of her week and the reason this was her favourite course from the degree programme.

The class fell silent as he strode to his uncluttered desk, which stood to the side, and placed his black leather satchel on the wooden surface. Without saying a word, he shrugged off the blazer of his charcoal two-piece suit and hung it over the back of the chair.

Enthralled and mouth dry, she watched the seductive movements of his tall, athletic body. Broad shoulders and wide chest, toned biceps and sturdy thighs lay concealed in the long-sleeved, sky blue shirt, navy tie, and achromatic trousers.

She imagined him being fit, not overly muscular. Yet, strong enough to sweep her into his arms and claim her in an age-old lovers' dance. Inexperienced in matters of the flesh, and with knowledge garnered from books alone, it didn't stop her mind from conjuring images of the two of them. He would spread her on his desk and pleasure her with his hands and mouth and body.

Her stomach clenched, and her nipples hardened.

She stifled a moan and shifted in her seat, glancing around surreptitiously in case anyone noticed her daydreaming about having sex with the lecturer.

No one paid her any attention, their focus on the man in question.

He was well-respected, by staff and students. His classes were always packed, and the female students, especially, made an extra effort on their appearances, including Isha.

She'd straightened her naturally kinky hair, keeping the locks smooth and shiny enough to reflect the fluorescent lights in the hall. She'd even applied makeup—lip gloss and mascara—although she wouldn't go as far as to put on the mini-dresses that some of her fellow students wore in class.

She'd opted for a black woollen turtleneck sweater dress that reached her knees, sheer tights, and black and red leather sneakers. Classic comfort was her preferred style since she was incognito.

Would he be tempted to have a clandestine affair with his student?

She'd heard rumours of lecturers who behaved in such manners. However, Professor Bassong had never been mentioned in any of the gossips.

Would he ever notice her? Was she headed for disappointment where he was concerned?

A heaviness settled in her chest, and for a moment, she struggled to breathe as she lowered her gaze to the desk. She twisted the flame-shaped ruby pendant hanging from a gold chain around her neck.

Grandma Mina had given her the heirloom for which she was named during her coming-of-age ritual. Each of the first daughters in the lineage was named after one of the jewels extracted from the Fumi family mines. Hence the reason her mother's name was Sapphire.

"I named you Ruby because you are full of passion and loyalty," Grandma Mina had said as she had placed the stone in Isha's palm. "This gem will bring you good fortune and pure love. Keep it with you at all times."

Now, Isha mouthed a prayer, "Bring me luck. Bring me love," and rubbed the ruby as if it had magical powers and could grant her wish.

Her desires would remain in her head, and no one would find out. Not even the man of her dreams. Her yearnings were fanciful at best and shameful at worst, according to Bagumi societal and imperial conventions.

Not only should she be of pure mind and body, but also, she wouldn't be able to do anything about it if she got noticed by the lecturer.

As the daughter of a mighty king, she could only date a strict selection of men to make a match that would strengthen the Kingdom of Bagumi.

Professor Bassong did not qualify for that concise list of powerful men.

He swivelled to face the class, his gaze sweeping over his audience. Mini-skirt or not, he didn't linger on any particular student or give anyone any extra attention.

He turned back to the table, opened the flap of the satchel, and pulled out items—a textbook, notepad, and marker pen. Then, he strode to the whiteboard and scribbled on it. *War and International Order.*

His movements were assured and measured as if he'd done them a thousand times before so that he had become finely attuned to the impact on his audience.

The class was still, silent, rapt in attention as they followed his actions.

Pride swelled her chest as she watched him. An African, just like she was, could command the attention of a theatre full of international students.

Known to be hard but fair, he expected a lot from his students. He didn't suffer fools, and everyone knew they only had one chance to be in his class. Otherwise, he would toss them out.

Professor Bassong might not be a king. Nonetheless, this classroom was his kingdom, and the students were his subjects.

Isha loved being one of his subjects, although he never bestowed any special recognition on her. She didn't mind sharing his limited time with others, as long as no one else snagged his interest.

Someone's phone vibrated loudly on a hard surface, and gasps and murmurs erupted in the hall.

Isha turned to find the girl sitting behind her in the next row scrambling to switch off and hide the offending object.

Too late, though.

"What is your name?" Professor Bassong's voice was stern and sharp enough to chop wood, or more specifically, to cut a misbehaving student to size.

The hairs on Isha's arms and neck stood erect at the tone of his formal British accent which reminded her of actor David Oyelowo's voice. And heat flared on her skin as if she was the one he addressed.

He stared straight at the young woman, his arms folded across his chest, his jaw set in a hard line, his clean-shaven chin jutting.

"Jenna ... My name is Jenna Hillman," the girl stammered, and lowered her head.

He reached in a drawer and pulled out a sheet of paper.

And then, he strode to the row of chairs and stopped in front of Isha.

Her pulse sky-rocketed and she licked her lips, tasting her cherry lip gloss.

He stood close enough to touch.

Her fingers tingled with the urge to graze the subtle check-patterned fabric of his charcoal trousers, to feel the warmth and hardness of corded thigh muscles underneath. She caught the scent of his spicy cologne. Definitely cedar wood, cloves, cinnamon, and something else she couldn't identify.

"Ms. Hillman, take this and read out the content." He passed the sheet of paper to Jenna.

Jenna's face fell as she started reading. "This is the code of conduct for the students attending the International Law and Order course."

She went on to outline the terms about punctuality, behaviour in class, phones and gadgets, and even dress code.

Isha knew the document mostly by heart as she had read it and abided by it. Most of the students did, but there were rare occasions like this when a mobile device went off in class, resulting in the culprit being subjected to humiliation by reading out the code of conduct.

It worked quite well because she had never witnessed repeat offenders.

When Jenna finished the reading, Professor Bassong took the sheet and returned it to his desk.

"Now that we have all been reminded of the student obligations, we shall get on with the topic for today." He turned to face the class. "Of the Four Horsemen of the Apocalypse named by John of Patmos in the Book of Revelations, which one of the Horsemen is the most avoidable? Anyone?"

Isha's heart thumped as she raised a clammy hand.

The professor's sharp, assessing gaze fell on her. "Ms ...?"

Her heart thumped harder, and her cheeks flushed as she lowered her hand to the top of the desk. This was the first time he'd addressed her since she started attending his class. "Bagumi. Ruby Bagumi."

"And the answer?" he said, his expression not changing.

There was no flicker of interest. No hint that being bestowed the knowledge of her full name filled him with excitement just as it energised her.

She swallowed the twinge of disappointment and ignored the tightness in her chest.

She had come prepared for this class, for him.

Like the rare occasion of being granted an audience with the monarch, she would make the most of his attention while she had it.

"War is the most avoidable of the four," she said in a clear voice, maintaining eye contact as butterflies fluttered in her chest.

"Explain your reasoning, Ms. Bagumi?" He leaned against the top to the chair with both hands. For the first time, he focused his gaze on her for more than fleeting seconds as if he had the desire to learn about her as well as what she had to say.

Her internal temperature increased along with her heartbeats. She swallowed the nerves threatening to kick in. She could do this.

"First of all, Death is inevitable for all of us. While we can prolong life through science and technology, the body is set to die from the moment one is born. Pestilence and Famine are largely unpreventable, although we can minimise their impact. But War?"

She shifted in the seat, passionate about her subject. She'd read up on the topic, determined to be noticed for her intelligence if her physical charms didn't work.

At home, excellence didn't make her stand out or get noticed. It was a standard expected of her as a member of the Royal House of Saene and the first daughter of the king.

Here, the university recognised and rewarded achievements with awards and accolades.

And she was determined to be noticed by her lecturer, this one in particular.

"War is avoidable," she continued. "Humans choose to wage war against other humans for tribal, racial, religious, and ultimately political power."

Someone in the back of the theatre scoffed.

Isha narrowed her eyes and clenched her teeth but refused to glance at the source of the interruption.

Professor Bassong looked in their direction. "Do you have something to say, Mr. Dodd?"

Joshua Dodd was one of those arrogant, smart-ass students who behaved as if he knew everything about the law because his father was a well-known Queen's Counsel, an eminent barrister appointed by the British monarch to be one of 'Her Majesty's learned in the law'. He was known for trying to paint other course-mates as fools.

"Ms. Bagumi implies that World Wars One and Two were avoidable, which is ridiculous." Joshua Dodd snickered.

"Ms. Bagumi, would you like to rebut?"

Professor Bassong's challenging gaze landed back on Isha. It was as if he was trying to figure out what kind of person she was—would she cower or fight back?

She straightened her shoulder and tilted her chin up, meeting his gaze without flinching.

She'd been raised to be a lioness, not a goat.

"Yes, Professor," she replied in a confident tone. "If we examine the causes of those unfortunate conflicts, we will find them to be rooted in imperialism and nationalism, which goes back to my earlier point that war is about political gain."

"Thank you, Ms. Bagumi." There was a hint of humour in his tone and sparkle in his ebony eyes as he bestowed her with the award she had craved since she'd first sat in his class—his acknowledgement.

Then his gaze swept the room again. "In this module, we explore the relations between war and international order. Is war a tool for keeping international order? Is it avoidable or not?"

As the rest of the lecture carried on, adrenaline rushed through Isha, rejuvenating her.

Her first love had noticed her. Finally.

Chapter Two

London, United Kingdom
February 2008

ISHA stepped out of the staff entrance onto the dark side alley. A grey outdoor lamp glowed dimly from the corner of the Bar Atlantic building. Fat drops of cold rain splattered onto her skin and the pavement.

"Great," she muttered. She'd forgotten her umbrella. She would be soaked through before she reached her destination.

Just what she needed after a long day. Not.

In a hurry, she navigated past stacks of water-stained crates, greasy-looking puddles, and the large metal industrial bins.

This was what she got for wanting to experience student life like any ordinary millennial.

A job that finished late at night, freezing rain, and bad days.

She puffed out a sigh.

What she wouldn't give, at this moment, for a minder with an umbrella ushering her into a warm, chauffeured car and taking her home. On days like this, she missed the luxurious comforts of being a regal princess.

An image of her father's stony expression flashed in her mind as his words registered. "*We'll see how long you're going to cope with student life without your royal privileges.*"

Her quest for independence had turned into a battle of wills with her parents.

Her father was noble and proud. The idea of one of his children living like a commoner was an irritation he would rather not endure. He hoped she would change her mind.

All Isha had to do was to make one phone call, and all her royal perks would be reinstated.

However, she was on a quest to explore the world and understand herself better. These years at university provided the best time to do so. Upon graduation, her life would be taken over by duty to her family and to the Kingdom of Bagumi.

Meanwhile, she had abandoned Her Royal Highness, Princess Isha Saene on the plane when she'd disembarked at Heathrow Airport over eighteen months ago and taken on the persona of Ruby Bagumi.

Ruby wasn't entitled to chauffeured cars or indulgent servants or excessive bank balances. She had to work to top up her student allowance if she wanted any extras beyond the necessary living expenses.

She pulled the collar of her coat as far up as possible, turned right onto the main street, and walked briskly towards Piccadilly. Green Park, the underground station she needed, was ten minutes in this direction.

On a warm, dry night, and when she had her flatmate and best friend, Amara, for company, she could do the forty minutes walk to their apartment in Pimlico. Not a good idea to attempt the walk alone at this late hour.

The other option would be to try to hail a black cab. However, that task could prove impossible in this weather. Catching the tube was the best option, and hopefully, she'd be home in twenty minutes.

After a hot shower, she could crawl into bed and forget the crappy day she'd experienced.

She'd barely trudged fifty yards through the downpour when the beam of lights from an approaching vehicle made her jump away from the edge of the pavement in the hopes of avoiding a splash of the dirty puddle.

"Ms. Bagumi?" a familiar masculine voice called out.

Isha froze, her heart jolting. She would recognise that sensual rumble anywhere, but she must have misheard with the rain and all.

Still, she turned to the sleek, black Audi TT parked by the pavement. Through the wound-down front window, the driver came into view. It was *him*!

Professor Bassong.

What was he doing here? She usually saw him once a week on Mondays in the lecture hall. She'd never encountered him outside of the university premises.

He stepped out of his car.

She moved backwards, wrapping her arms around her body as she tried to slow her racing pulse.

He came around, raindrops splashing on this blazer, soaking him. He didn't seem to care as he held the passenger door open. "Get in the car."

She shook her head and took another step away. She didn't make a habit of getting into men's cars, although this one was hardly a stranger.

"Thank you. But the tube station is not that far."

She could kick herself, though. Professor Bassong, the man who had taken up a leading role in her salacious dreams, the man who was totally out of bounds to her, offered her a lift, and she was turning him down? What was wrong with her?

In all of her fantasies, she hadn't envisioned an encounter with him while drenched like a cat dragged out of the River Thames. She must look horrid in her current state—wet hair plastered to her face while water dripped down her clothes.

"Ms. Bagumi, you'll catch a cold in this weather. Let me take you home."

She recognised the challenge in his tone above the howling wind. He was really saying 'are we going to stand out here and debate the benefits of getting a lift?'

He spoke the truth. Her body still hadn't acclimatised to the changeable British weather. A few more minutes out here, and she would be sneezing and coughing for days.

Hadn't she been the one praying for a chauffeured limousine a short while ago?

Although she hadn't expected the prayer to be answered by the sexy professor in his sporty coupé, she would be foolish to decline.

"Alright. Thank you," she replied and hurried into the car, sinking into the warm leather bucket seat with a sigh of relief.

He joined her and shut the door as she clicked her harness into place.

"Where are you headed?" he asked.

She told him, and he keyed the address into the console of the satellite navigation, long fingers flicking the controls. Then, he drove down to the end of the street and turned right at the traffic lights, onto the main road heading south-west.

Warm air blew out of the vents, taking the chill off her skin. Her pulse raced, and her chest tingled.

In the months since he'd been her lecturer, she had been content to attend his classes and observe him from across the room. She participated in class, asking and answering questions. They'd gotten the results of Semester One examinations this week, and she had done very well on all the subjects.

In all that time, they hadn't been in a one-to-one situation.

Now, she sat in Professor Bassong's car, only a few inches from him. They hadn't made any physical contact, but she could reach out and touch him.

She stared at her wet hands. Touching was not a good idea. Nope.

Water dripped from her hair, packed in a bunch with an elastic band. She grimaced. She would damage the seat with her damp clothes.

"I'm really sorry about your car," she murmured. "Perhaps you should've left me to walk."

"And let you catch a cold? No." He glanced at her, his expression too intense in the unlit interior.

Was he concerned? Or did she observe something more profound in his eyes?

"True. But it shouldn't matter to you whether I catch a cold or not," she stated, as the hope of something more than fleeting flared inside her.

"Of course it matters. If you catch a cold, then you are likely to miss my classes. And that's not good. You've had a hundred per cent attendance record so far. You can't ruin it."

Shoulders slumped, she fiddled with the buckle of her tote and let out a sigh. "Oh."

His only concern was her attendance in his class?

Why did she wish for more from him?

He seemed to have picked up on her dismay and looked at her again. "And you are my most engaged student. I have to come to each class prepared with my A-game. You keep me on my toes."

Wow. High praise from her professor. He might as well have lauded her as the best student or even the most crucial person in the world.

A grin spread on her face as warmth radiated through her body. "Thank you, Professor Bassong."

"You're welcome." The lines around his eyes softened, and his mouth curled up.

Hot damn. He was more handsome when he smiled, even from a side profile.

And those sensuous lips of his—how would they feel on hers, on her neck, on her breasts?

She relaxed, her body melting with the fantasy, desire tingling along her nerve endings.

Hot for him, even watching him as he turned a dial mesmerised her.

The soulful voice of Asa came through the speakers as she sang '360' from her debut album which had been released recently.

"I love this song," she said before she could stop. She enjoyed every song on the groundbreaking album.

"You do?" He sounded amused.

"Yes. Every track in the album. It's my favourite. I practically have it on a loop in my music player," she rambled. "I can't believe you listen to the same songs as I do."

Was it serendipity that they shared a love of this type of music?

"Why not? Because I'm old and not hip enough?" His black eyes sparkled with humour.

"No. You're not old." Well, he was older than her by ten years. She'd read his impressive biography.

He'd been born in Wanai, West Africa, a PhD holder and a successful lawyer in his own right. He spoke English, French, Ganui, and Wanai. His father had been a Chief Justice of the Supreme Courts. Unfortunately, he had died in a fatal accident a few years ago. His mother was a lecturer and a well-known women's rights activist.

"I mean you're young and sexy and attractive, you can listen to whatever you like ..." she rattled on until she realised what she'd just said. "Oh my goodness. I'm sorry. I didn't mean that, Professor Bassong."

"You didn't mean that I was young and sexy and attractive?" His chuckle rumbled in the car.

She would've enjoyed the deep merry sound from him if she wasn't currently dying of embarrassment.

"No ... Umm ... Yes. Oh, Lord." She covered her face with her hands. "I'm so sorry."

"Don't be. And thank you for the compliment." He didn't sound offended.

She dropped her hands and peeked in his direction.

His lips were still curled upwards as he drove into another street.

She recognised the houses in her neighbourhood. The rain downpour had slowed to a light drizzle.

"You can stop here," she said, eager to escape. Perhaps he wouldn't remember what she'd meant by the time she saw him again at the next class.

"No. I'll walk you to your door. It's too late at night for you to be on your own," he replied in a firm tone. The same tone he used in class.

She didn't argue. Better to just keep her mouth shut in case she said something else outrageous.

He drove past her apartment building in search of a parking space and found one a block down.

Hands trembling, she pulled her bunch from the tote and unclipped her seatbelt as he climbed out.

Before she could reach for the handle, he opened the door.

"Thank you," she said in surprise. No one had done anything chivalrous for her since her arrival in the U.K.

His gallantry didn't end there as he ascended the steps to the entrance of the block of flats, waited for her to unlock the latch and held the slab for her to walk in.

"I'll be fine now," she said, not wanting to be any more trouble.

"I said I'll walk you to your door. There have been incidents of people being attacked in communal areas like this."

A smile curled her lips as she walked up the stairs.

He reminded her of overprotective older brothers, Zawadi especially, who didn't want her in London without twenty-four-hour security.

"Do you always finish work this late?" Professor Bassong asked as he followed her.

She glanced back in surprise. "How did you know I was working?"

"I was in Bar Atlantic with a friend. I saw you serving drinks."

He'd been there? She stopped when she reached the entrance to her flat. "Oh. I didn't see you."

He placed his hands in his trouser pockets and held her gaze. "I was in the VIP section upstairs."

Her mouth fell open as a gasp escaped. "VIP?"

She didn't serve the exclusive members' area as it catered for clients with peculiar requirements. She'd been curious but not brave enough to actually request a change on the rota.

"Yes," he said, his gaze piercing. "Have you ever been up there?"

"No. Of course not," she replied quickly. "I only work downstairs in the main club."

Since he was a VIP member, did that mean he was one of those with peculiar requirements?

Had he been with someone else tonight? She crossed her arms over her chest, burning with jealousy as she stared at his face to figure out if he had.

His expression stayed unreadable. "So do you finish at this time every shift?"

"More or less. I work only on Friday nights." She answered with a pinched expression, still unsettled about the possibility of him with someone else.

"It seems reasonable, although I don't think walking through dark alleys alone at this time of night is a good thing."

"I'm usually not alone. My friend Amara who is also my flatmate works at Bar Atlantic, too. But she is away on a Valentine weekend to Paris."

Yesterday had been Valentine's Day. Had Professor Bassong spent it alone?

She wanted to ask him, but it was inappropriate. Him giving her a lift didn't give her license over his life.

Her discrete investigations had revealed him to be single and available, which had excited her. She had fantasised about him waiting for a suitable time when their love for each other could be revealed.

However, she hadn't prepared for him dating others.

Her stomach hardened, and black spots formed in her vision.

Stupid. She had no claim over him. She was forbidden from getting involved with him.

Try telling that to her heart which had become set on him from the moment she'd seen him walk into the lecture hall for the first time.

She wanted to arrogate him and put a tag on him that read 'Keep off. Property of Isha.'

"Okay. If you open your door, I can go." He pointed his right thumb over his shoulder in the direction they'd just come.

"Of course." She put the key in her lock, and it popped open. "Thank you."

"You're welcome," he replied. "Good night, Ms. Bagumi."

"Good night, Professor." She stepped into her apartment and turned around.

His footsteps thudded as he walked back towards the stairs.

"Professor," she called out, feeling like she had to do something. Tonight was the closest she'd been to him all year. Perhaps, this was her only chance to seduce him. "Would you like to come in for a cup of coffee?"

He turned around, hands in his pockets. "No. Thank you, Ms. Bagumi. Perhaps another time."

"Of course." Her cheeks heated, and she shut the door and leaned against it, eyes closed.

What did she know about seducing an older man, anyway? She had no experience.

So why couldn't she let go of this taboo attraction she had towards her lecturer?

CHAPTER THREE

LONDON, UNITED KINGDOM
MARCH 2008

ZAIN Bassong didn't get to his station in life by giving in to whims.

He excelled as an academic because he prepared, researched, analysed, wrote papers, and never stopped exploring and expanding his knowledge. As a lawyer, he was personable, persuasive, and persistent. He had empathy for others and could read people.

He was principled—didn't drink alcohol or smoke cigarettes or take drugs. He obeyed the laws and paid his taxes. He loved his family and cared for his community.

Still, he had desires that some would judge as depraved and immoral. Yearnings that had become complicated since the start of this school year. Since a certain young lady had become his student.

He killed the engine of his car once he'd pulled into a parking spot. He climbed out and strode the fifty or so yards out of the underground lot, down a short street to the nondescript grey metal door with the embossed Bar Atlantic logo.

A uniformed doorman greeted him as he tapped his membership card on the electronic scanner. As a VIP, he could visit the establishment and avoid the crowds at the main entrance while ensuring his relative anonymity.

Blue lights gave the dark-hued walls of the foyer an electric look while the thumping baseline from the House music coming from the ground floor vibrated beneath the soles of his black Italian brogues.

He took the stairs to the upper level where another hefty uniformed guard let him into the VIP lounge with a smile and a nod. As soon as the door shut behind him, it seemed he had stepped into a different place.

R-n-B music played low from the speakers, Missy Elliot rapping in her latest release 'Ching-A-Ling.' The coloured lighting continued in here but didn't flicker like downstairs, adding to the ambience. A bar counter with a colourful display of bottles, glass, and shelving stood at one end while a small dance floor occupied the other end. In the middle, there were sofas for comfort and booths for privacy, allowing for guests to sit and chat.

A glass wall gave a view of the crowded nightclub below.

Zain made an effort not to look at the glass wall as he made his way across the hard grey floor.

It had been about four weeks since he'd last been in here. Four weeks since he'd discovered that Ruby Bagumi worked here after he'd spied her through the glass wall.

In class, he could maintain the professional distance, although seeing her during the International Law and Order seminars had become the main feature of his work week.

Ruby was smart and beautiful and easily one of the most tuned-in students he'd taught. She asked probing questions that challenged his world view as well as gave reasoned answers that showed she prepared for each class as much as any student should.

Unlike some other students who sought one-on-one attention from him after the lectures, she had never requested alone time with him.

And he had never sought her out.

Until that night a month ago when he'd seen her through the two-way glass of the VIP lounge as he watched the revellers below. She had been in the staff uniform, serving drinks to the partygoers. He'd had to ask the bar manager what time her shift would end. Afterwards, he'd waited in his car hoping he would catch her.

Luckily for him, the great British weather had worked in his favour, and she'd had little choice but to get in his car when he'd offered to drive her home.

Sitting in that car, he'd pictured himself taking her wet clothes off and warming her up with his body heat.

Such were inappropriate thoughts he shouldn't entertain, and he had kept his hands to himself even after she'd told him he was 'young and sexy and attractive' or when she'd invited him into her home for coffee. The invitation to coffee seemed to be an invitation to more, especially at that hour of the night. Still, some lines shouldn't be crossed.

Ms. Bagumi was a temptation he had to avoid.

Bar Atlantic had provided a refuge, a diversion from his true desires, the fulfilment of pleasure.

Before he'd discovered her employment as a waitress here, he'd been able to choose other willing sexual partners as her replacement. Perverse as that might seem, the fantasy had worked.

However, the last few weekends, he hadn't been able to come back here knowing she would only be metres away and within reach. Knowing he could invite her to his table. Knowing they could chat. Knowing her company would set fire to his veins.

But he couldn't keep away forever.

He wasn't a saint.

And he didn't want to risk a situation where he sought her out beyond the classroom like he'd done the last time.

Now, he had to refocus on finding the person who would assuage his desires for the night.

He chose a leather armchair in a dark corner that had another chair adjacent which could come in handy if he decided he wanted company. For now, it was enough to browse.

Guests already made use of the facilities, the right mix of men and women.

Executives, professional athletes, and celebrities—people who needed the discretion and exclusivity but still wanted to enjoy the company of someone who shares the same tastes as they did for the night without strings attached.

A waitress approached with a smile and a cheerful voice. "Good evening, sir. Can I get you anything?"

"Hello, Amara—" He read her name tag pinned to the black vest. "Please get me a bottled Coke and no ice in the glass."

He was always specific about what he wanted. Otherwise, they assumed he wanted ice and the drink from the tap.

"Of course." She smiled as she scribbled on her notepad and hurried away.

He leaned back into his seat as a dark-skinned woman in a fitted plum sleeveless dress and stilettos walked over to him.

"Hello, Zain," she said with a hint of a French accent.

"Kari, how are you?" He stood and kissed her on the cheeks.

"I'm good. May I join you?" Karidja—or Kari for short—Dembélé had been born in France to Senegalese parents. She worked for an investment bank in the City of London.

They'd met over a year ago at the newly opened club and had hit it off. They had overlapping tastes, so sometimes hooked up when they were in the venue at the same time.

Tonight, he wasn't in the mood to explain his requirements to a newbie, so Kari would fit the bill.

"Sure. Take a seat." He waved at the empty armchair. "Would you like a drink?"

As a rule, he wouldn't interact with a woman who was drunk or high. Strange, considering he sat in a nightclub where many people equated alcohol and drugs to fun times.

He had enough self-discipline to avoid substances that would cloud his judgement. And as a lawyer, what could seem like consent in a drunken state could be something different when one was clear-headed.

Ms. Dembélé had only just arrived, and she appeared sober. But he wouldn't take it any further if she ordered an alcoholic drink, a clear indication she only wanted to chat.

"Yes, please." She lowered her body into the lounge chair and placed her purse on the side table.

He raised his hand to attract attention and froze.

A waitress carried a silver tray of drinks towards him.

Not Amara, the one who had taken his order.

This one with the black skirt that hugged her wide hips, black vest, a white shirt covering ample breasts, and brunette Afro hair pinned back in a bunch he would recognise anywhere. If he had any doubts, the name written on her tag confirmed his suspicion.

"Good evening, sir. Your drink," Ruby Bagumi said in a calm voice as she placed the bottle of Coke on the table along with the empty glass.

A flush of adrenaline tingled through his body at her proximity.

She stood close enough to touch, close enough to caress.

He hadn't planned on seeing her tonight. Certainly not up here. Hadn't she said that she only worked downstairs? Having her here brought complications. He was trying to forget about her, damn it. Why did she have to invade this sanctuary, as well?

He took in a deep breath, and her scent invaded his nostrils.

Damn. She smelled of flowers and musk.

His fingers itched to reach out and tug her closer so he could bury himself in her seductive scent. Instead, he tightened his grip on the arm of his chair.

"Will that be all?" she asked, chin tilted and jaw tightened.

Her tone lacked the humility or cheerfulness displayed by other staff. Poised like a queen, she stared at a point above his head as if they were inconsequential citizens in her realm.

He'd seen similar responses from her in school. Whenever one of the other students tried to treat her with disdain in class, the fearless lioness would appear and take him down a peg or two.

Not understanding the reason for Ruby's current disposition, he chose to ignore it. Moreover, he couldn't ask her directly. He shouldn't show any familiarity with her.

He glanced at Kari and nodded, giving permission for the woman to order what she wanted.

"I'll have the cola drink, as well, but with ice," Kari said.

"Okay." Ruby turned and walked away.

His gaze followed her swaying hips across the lounge.

"That waitress has an attitude."

Kari's harsh voice drew his attention.

"She's probably new," he said in Ruby's defence.

The waitress had snubbed Kari by not greeting her, which was rude and not the kind of behaviour to be displayed in the venue unless she was begging to be disciplined.

Unbidden, an image of Ruby spread across his lap, filled his mind.

His fingers tingled, and he curled them into balls.

He wasn't going there.

She was out of bounds. Forbidden. Illicit. Prohibited.

How many more synonyms did he need to remind him of the futility of his desires?

"She won't last long here if she continues with the insolent behaviour," Kari sniped. "I have the mind to report her."

His chest burned, and his stomach hardened.

The rules of the members' lounge were different.

If Kari complained, Ruby would be punished. By someone else.

His protective instincts rolled with the flash of jealousy.

He would break his rules first before he'd let anyone else in this lounge touch Ruby.

Damn it. She shouldn't be up here.

"No, Kari. Don't," he ordered, turning to meet her gaze. "I'll handle the waitress."

"Sure." She nodded.

Eager to take his mind away from the student, he poured some Coke into the glass and lifted it. "So, tell me. How are things going with you?"

She sighed. "Not so good. The City is crazy at the moment with all the banks collapsing. It's as if every new day brings more bad news in the financial markets. So I really need to not think about work tonight."

"Was there any specific things you were interested in?"

She was always good at laying out her needs, which made his job so much easier. This wasn't the night for self-discovery.

"I want to feel out of control and to be made to submit. I want to be dominated and used hard. But most of all, I want to get out of my head."

As he listened to her lay out what she needed, his mind drifted to the waitress. How would Ruby feel about losing control, about being dominated by him?

"Does that work for you?" Kari reached out and stroked his arm.

He didn't have time to respond before Ruby returned with Kari's drink and dumped it on the table with a thud.

The final straw.

He jaw tightened. "Ruby, apologise to Ms. Karidja immediately, or I'll be forced to take you across my knees and spank you arse here and now."

The leader in him couldn't resist the call to duty, to correct an errant behaviour, especially in his ... student. She was his student. Full stop. He wouldn't tolerate a bad attitude at the university. He wouldn't accept it here.

Ruby was intelligent enough to understand and be cautious, considering their location.

Her eyes widened, and her mouth fell open. She took a step back.

"What? You can't do that?" she said in a shaky, halting voice.

"Did you read and sign the regulations for the members' lounge before you began working here?" he asked in the same stern voice he used in class.

Her throat bobbed as she swallowed. She shifted from one foot to the other. "Yes, I did."

If they were in the lecture hall, he'd make her read aloud from the Student's Code of Conduct as a reminder.

"What is rule number three?" he asked, hoping for her sake she remembered. Otherwise, he'd make her get a copy of the house regulations and read them out.

Her forehead creased. "Wait-staff will be courteous at all times."

Good girl.

It seemed she'd memorised the list.

His chest swelled with pride as if she genuinely was *his* good girl.

"And what is rule number five?" he probed.

"Members can administer appropriate punishment to unruly wait-staff in the form of, and no more than, ten hard spanks to the bottom."

"Good. So you know naughty girls get punished. A spanking or an apology, which will it be, Ruby?" He rolled her name around his tongue, relishing the promise encased in the caution.

He didn't create the house regulations. Still, he'd enforce them where she was concerned.

She swallowed again and glanced around the room as if expecting someone to come to her rescue.

No one would interfere unless she protested. Even then, she'd land into deeper water with her boss if Kari complained about her conduct.

With the round silver tray clutched to her chest as if it would protect her, she lowered her gaze to the floor and said. "I'm sorry, madam. I didn't mean to be rude."

She'd done the right thing. He should be relieved.

Still, as much as he shouldn't touch her, he could not help the disappointment tightening his chest. He kept his hard gaze on her for a few more seconds before turning to the woman beside him, "Kari?"

"I accept your apology. But you better be on your best fucking—"

"Language," he cut her off in warning.

"I'm sorry," Kari muttered as she picked up her drink.

He nodded and turned back to Ruby. "That will be all."

"Thank you, sir," she said and scurried away.

If she had any sense, she would go back to working in the dance club and never come back to the VIP lounge.

He picked up his drink and downed it in one gulp, hoping to chase away the heat on his skin at the image playing over and over in his mind.

Of Ruby Bagumi bent over his lap. His to play with. His to love.

Chapter Four

THE next morning, Isha dragged her lethargic body out of bed, lured by the aroma of freshly brewed coffee.

Sunlight came through the large windows into the open-plan living space, which included the dining and kitchen at one end. The interior retained the original high ceilings of the Georgian architecture although the rest of the flat had been modernised to a contemporary design.

"You finally woke up." Amara sat on a high stool, flicking the pages of a textbook on the granite top of the breakfast bar and scribbling on a notebook with a black and gold roller-ball pen. A half-empty white porcelain mug sat on a juniper wood disc.

Isha glanced at the wall clock with matte grey edge and crisp white dial. The long metal hand was almost at ten while the short one was close to twelve.

The late shifts at Bar Atlantic meant she had a lie-in on Saturday mornings. However, she was usually up before eleven a.m.

"Yeah," she mumbled as she went over to cupboard and took out another mug.

The counter had been wiped down, and all the dishes put away. Amara was one of the most organised people she knew, partly why they got along. Neither had to worry about each other's messes because they liked to keep the flat they shared spotless.

Isha poured coffee and scooped in Demerara sugar before topping it with milk from the fridge. The spoon tinkled as she stirred the drink. She dumped the spoon in the sink and swivelled to make her way back to her room.

"What happened last night?" Amara's tone was curious.

Isha wasn't in the mood for conversation. "Nothing."

She just wanted to crawl back into bed, drink coffee, and wallow in self-pity.

"Nothing? That's all you're going to say after you messed up?" Amara wasn't going to let this go.

Puffing out a sigh, Isha carried the drink over to the counter next to her friend. She climbed onto a stool and took a sip of coffee. Within seconds, the caffeine and sugar combo boosted her. No matter the shitstorm erupting in her life, she could be guaranteed a cup of quality Java.

One of the perks of sharing this two-bed residence with her bestie who happened to also be the only daughter of a Nigerian king. Yes, Amara was another royal princess. An encounter in a Swiss preparatory school had bonded them for life.

When Isha had suggested that they go incognito at university, her best friend had jumped at the chance. They had both plotted on how to convince their parents.

However, while Isha's father still hated the idea and had restricted her access to funds as a deterrent, Amara's parents subsidised her student life. Her friend had always been daddy's girl.

When they'd decided the area of London they wanted to live in, Amara's father had bought the building containing their flat. The place had been refurbished and furnished for them. They lived rent-free, although they had to pay other bills and feed themselves.

Amara had found them the jobs at Bar Atlantic through her Nigerian connections.

So Isha owed her an explanation about last night, at the very least.

Her friend continued scribbling on the notepad.

Isha took another sip and returned her mug to the wooden coaster. "I messed up."

Amara sighed, dropped her pen on the table, and glanced over. "You did. You know I had to beg the boss to let you work up at the VIP Lounge, and you go and pull a stunt like that. What came over you?"

"It was that freaking woman!" All of last night's rollercoaster emotions came crashing down on Isha.

She pushed off the stool, causing it to scuff on the marble floor. She paced to the window. Her body trembled, and she clutched her midriff, caught between wanting to scream and wanting to cry.

After her encounter with Professor Bassong in the car when he'd brought her home weeks ago, she had begged Amara to get her on the Members' Lounge rota.

Her friend had always mentioned how she loved working there because there were fewer crowds, better tips, and intriguing guests. She'd also warned Isha about the house regulations. "Nothing that happens there can be discussed outside."

Eventually, Isha had been summoned to the owner's office where he'd confirmed that she could work at the lounge on a trial basis.

Last night, she'd been assigned to serve a section of the bar while Amara had another part. Butterflies had fluttered in her belly when she'd seen Professor Bassong arrive. However, he'd chosen a seat in Amara's section, and Isha had had to beg her friend to swap so she could serve him.

Before she'd delivered his drink, a female guest had wiggled her way to chat with him.

Mildly irritated, she'd served the drink to him, hoping he'd acknowledge her.

He hadn't. Not even a smile.

They'd shared a few private moments in his car. Didn't she deserve a 'hello, Ruby' or 'how are you, Ruby' or 'I missed you, Ruby'?

Okay, that last one was highly improbable.

Still, her irritation had snowballed at his snub, first to disappointment and finally to rage when the Kari woman had touched the professor.

The memory made her body overheat, and she scrubbed her palms over her face.

"Unnh," she growled and planted her head on the window pane, arms dangling.

Cold hands landed on her shoulders and massaged the knotted muscles. "Girl, take a deep breath and tell me what's going on. Didn't you like working at the VIP Lounge?"

She sighed, lifted her head, and walked back to the stool. "I did. At first."

After reading and signing a contract that included a non-disclosure agreement to serve drinks at the exclusive bar, she had expected weird stuff like orgies or whatever to happen last night.

However, the VIP guests had enjoyed themselves, drinking, chatting, and dancing. They appeared a little different from the rest of the revellers. Some exuded dark, unyielding authority, setting her pulse alight. She'd seen the total attention they'd paid their companions, and she'd wanted the same thing.

She'd been polite, deferent, and had served drinks or food as ordered.

"Then, what happened?" Amara's voice pulled her out of her reverie. "You asked me to swap places, so you could serve Mister Zain, and then afterwards, you shut yourself in the ladies'. And then, Mister K called you in for a chat. Did he do something to you?"

"No!" She shook her head and sucked in a heavy breath before saying in a quiet voice. "He threatened to spank me."

"Who did? Mister K?" Amara gasped.

"No. Professor Bassong." A shiver slid down her spine as she remembered the harsh tone of his voice and his hardened expression.

"You know he is Mister Zain at Bar Atlantic. You can't call him Professor Bassong."

"I know." She didn't care. He would always be Professor Bassong to her. Her professor. The man who had taken up nightly residence in her dreams. The man she'd set her heart on.

Until last night.

Her lungs constricted, making it hard to breathe.

"Why did he want to punish you?" Amara probed.

Isha swallowed with difficulty and tipped her head back. "I may have been rude to his companion—" She flapped her hand "—Ms. Karidja or whatever her name was."

"That attitude *will* get you a spanking," her flatmate commented as she lifted both brows, body jerking.

"She had no right to touch him." Her fury returned, seeping into her voice.

"It is a night club. Men and women go there to hook up."

"Not him."

"Hang on a minute. Are you having an affair with Professor Bassong?"

"No, I'm not having an affair with him. That's the point. He's doing it with the Kates, Karens, and Karidjas that turn up at Bar Atlantic instead."

She tossed her arms in the air, hopped off the stool, and stalked to the window again.

She hadn't known it would hurt so much to find out that the lecturer was dating other women. Seeing him with that woman had broken something inside Isha last night, no matter how irrational it seemed.

Her chest felt tight. She fought not to crumble, and clutched her arms around her midriff.

Amara didn't say anything for a few minutes, probably shocked by Isha's outburst.

Then, she joined her by the window and spoke in a soft voice. "You're in love with him?"

Isha swallowed but still couldn't speak without breaking down. She glanced at her friend as tears filled her eyes and nodded.

"Oh, sweetie. I'm so sorry." Amara wrapped her arms around Isha's shoulders and hugged her. "I didn't know."

She stepped back to wipe her face with both palms. "I didn't know how much I wanted him until I saw him with that woman. The way she touched him just blew a fuse in my head."

She turned back to the window but not really seeing outside. Instead, her view was of the bar, Professor Bassong and the woman sitting side by side, talking intimately.

"Why her? Why not me? Is it because she is skinny, and I'm not?"

The self-recrimination had started last night. Perhaps she needed to sign up for a gym membership like Amara, who was there at least twice a week.

"Don't say that. You're gorgeous," her friend enthused.

Isha shrugged. "Or maybe it's because she's older and more experienced. She freaking knows how to seduce a man a whole lot better than I do."

She'd failed in her attempt to woo the professor, abysmally.

"Or it could be simply because he is your lecturer and you're his student. Anything else would be inappropriate," her friend tried to be the voice of reason.

"But the other day, he drove me home when it was raining. He walked me to the door." She pointed in the direction. "Doesn't that count for something?"

"He was just nice. We both have enough older brothers to know how overprotective they can get. It doesn't mean they want to date us."

"Well, I thought he cared about me. A man who cares wouldn't shove another woman in my face."

"That's a little unfair. Don't you think? He didn't know you were going to be there."

"Okay. Maybe he didn't know. Still ..." She rubbed her palms over her face and took a deep breath. "I wish I hadn't asked to work at the Members' Lounge. I really wish I didn't know he was having sex with other women because now, everything is ruined."

"Sweetie." Amara placed her hand on Isha's shoulder. "I think it is better you found out. At least, now you know you can get over the crush and move on."

"You're right. It's time to move on," Isha said even though she didn't believe it. She turned away, picked up her cold coffee, and dumped the liquid into the sink. Then, she washed out the mug and placed it on the drainer.

She'd taken the job at the VIP lounge to make the professor fall in love with her just as she was in love with him. He hadn't even given her a chance. He'd broken her heart. What would be the point in punishing herself more?

Bad enough when she would have to sit through his seminars for the rest of the year. On the upside, she didn't have to face him in class for another few weeks as they were on Easter break.

"I asked Mister K if I could go back to my old rota. He said I could," she spoke in a matter of fact tone.

"Well, that's good. At least, you still have a job. I thought he would've fired you."

"I thought so, too ... There's something about last night that I can't seem to get out of my mind."

"What is it?"

"At that moment when Prof—Mister Zain—threatened to spank me and demanded an apology, it was as if I had a connection with him. As if he saw me. It was a brief moment. But he acknowledged me. My pulse thumped, my heart soared while my belly did flip-flops. It was amazing and scary at the same time."

"Wow." Amara covered her wide smile with a hand.

"I know. I want to experience that feeling again."

"Not with Mister Zain, though."

"Of course not. That ship has sailed." Her chest tightened again.

"I'll be forced to take you across my knees and spank you arse here and now." She replayed the professor's words as her stomach muscles contracted and her clit pulsed.

"Another question." She leaned against the counter. "Have any of the VIP guests ever spanked you?"

Amara laughed. "Of course not. Then again, I don't go looking for trouble. I behave myself."

"But what if you get into trouble and one of them spanks you?"

Amara lifted her shoulders and dropped them. "If it happens, it happens."

"You don't mind? I mean, my father never spanked us as children. Why would I want to get spanked as a grown adult?"

"Because it is sexy," Amara answered with a wink.

Isha's mouth dropped open.

"Don't look so surprised." Her friend giggled. "The thrill of the possibilities is the reason I work there. Maybe when I find my own hot, sexy Dominant, I can misbehave so he can spank me."

"You're not serious." Isha gaped at her friend.

"I so am. In the meantime, we'll both keep away from the forbidden men. They are bad news."

"What do you mean 'forbidden men'?" She moved close to Amara. "Is there something you're not telling me?"

"It's nothing." Her flatmate went back to scribbling on the notepad.

Isha grabbed Amara's textbook. "I told you my secret. You have to tell me yours."

"Okay. Okay. Give me back the textbook, and I'll tell you."

Chapter Five

London, United Kingdom
May 2008

"*A PERSON will be remembered for his or her actions rather than intentions.*"

Those words from Zain's late father had formed the foundations for his life, and they stayed on his mind as he strode into the Bar Atlantic's members' lounge.

Good intentions. He'd had plenty of those.

Snubbing Ruby and threatening to spank her the night she'd served him two months ago had been driven by a worthy purpose.

He'd intended for her to stop working at the VIP bar because nothing good could come from seeing her every Friday night coupled with their weekly encounters in class. How long would he have been able to resist her? How long before he would have embroiled himself in something dangerously illicit?

His plan had worked.

Ruby had returned to serving drinks at the dance club. He hadn't seen her up here since then.

"Good evening, sir," the barman greeted when he approached. "What can I get you?"

"Evening, Ryan." He read the man's nametag pinned to his black vest. "Is Ruby working tonight?"

"Yes, sir. I believe she's on the lower floor."

"Please arrange for her to come up here. I'd like her to serve me tonight."

One of the perks of being a member was that he could choose his wait staff as long as he or she was on duty and available.

"Of course, sir. If you take a seat, I'll send her to you."

"Thank you." Zain headed across the lounge and exchanged greetings with other members he recognised.

When he reached his favourite armchair in the corner, he removed his suit jacket and hung it on the chrome rack to his right. He paid extra above his membership fee to reserve this particular seat because of its unrestricted view of the party floor below.

For the past two months since the incident with Ruby in the bar, he'd come here and sat in this chair every Friday night.

The first time had been surprisingly excruciating when he couldn't find her in the VIP Lounge or downstairs. He'd been worried that she might have lost her job until the bar manager had informed him that she'd gone away on holiday. Of course, he'd forgotten about the school break.

The next weekend, he'd been back and had puffed out a relieved breath on seeing her balancing a tray of empty bottles as she sashayed to the staff exit.

His relief had been short-lived.

On the first day of lectures after the holiday, he'd walked into the hall, carried out his usual routine—satchel down, jacket off, writing on the board, sweeping the theatre with his gaze—and his heart had stopped.

Ruby hadn't been sitting in the front row as usual.

Where is she? Did something happen to her? Worry had rippled through him as he'd scanned the row again.

When she didn't materialise in the designated spot, heart pounding in his chest, he'd scanned the rest of the room.

And found her sitting in the last row with all the latecomers and timewasters.

Any respite he'd felt by discovering her alive and well and in attendance had been overtaken by annoyance.

What the fuck is she doing back there?

She had a pen in her hand, and it moved across the notebook on the desk, her body leaning forward.

He'd stared at her for seconds longer than he would normally.

As if she'd sensed him, she'd defiantly lifted her head and held his gaze before averting her eyes.

In those couple of heartbeats that their gazes had connected, everything had become apparent. He'd read her fiery emotions, seen the depth of her anger directed at him.

He'd understood and allowed them to wash over him.

She'd wanted something—him—and he hadn't obliged her.

The cues had been there right from the start of the year. He'd ignored them the same way he'd ignored all the other students covertly seeking more than he would give.

However, the night he'd given her a lift home, something had changed between them.

First of all, he'd broken his rule. He'd shown some interest in his student even if it could be brushed off as harmless.

Ruby could have misread his intentions.

She'd invited him in for coffee, and by doing so, had laid her cards on the table.

She'd wanted him.

When he'd seen her in the Members' Lounge, she'd been there because of him, which would explain her reaction to Karidja's presence.

Still, he hadn't caved in, couldn't allow sentiments to overrule his judgement.

No matter how upset she'd seemed, he'd done the right thing by not indulging the attraction between them. Hadn't he?

He shook his head as he remembered everything that had happened since that night. Concern burned his heart, making him want to rub his chest.

It seemed his once great idea had unleashed a hellion.

Ruby's rebellion had gotten progressively worse.

She never returned to the front row, and she stopped engaging in class.

She refused to look him in the eyes, refused to volunteer for anything or participate in the class debates.

Tired of the silent treatment, he had forced her hand by asking her a direct question once.

She'd glared at him as she's answered.

Her fury had burned through him, providing a balm to his troubled soul at hearing her voice in class after several months of her reticence.

He hadn't realised he would miss her engagement in his class so much.

Still, he'd noticed her protests for attention and had ignored them.

She wasn't his to protect or cherish, never mind that his gut twisted at the thought.

Their brief encounter in the car months ago didn't translate to anything beyond what it had been—a man helping a young lady caught in bad weather.

During his visits, instead of interacting with other guests, he'd settled for watching Ruby through the Perspex as she went about her duties at the club.

Her hair was always pulled back in a bunch. The staff wore white shirts and black vests with black trousers or skirts. Although they were supposed to be uniform, her clothes moulded her curves in the most alluring way. Some wore their skirts a lot shorter than she did.

He had eyes for her alone.

On many occasions, he'd imagined moulding the flesh of her bare breasts and bum cheeks with his palm. Pictured mapping out every mound and crevice of her body with his mouth and hands.

Once he'd conjured up the image of her spread across his lap, he'd yearned for it to become a reality even when he'd known doing so would break one of his principles.

Barely functioning, she'd become an obsession he couldn't possess.

At least at the club, he breathed the same air as she did.

Utter madness.

Then this week, she'd done something worse.

Something he couldn't ignore.

Now, his heart raced and his mouth dried as he waited, knowing he'd see her soon.

What if she didn't show up?

For the first time since he'd made the decision to speak to Ruby at the club, uncertainty rippled through him.

What if she didn't want to see him?

How far would he go to talk to her?

He might have read the situation wrong.

No coercion. He wouldn't force her into his presence.

Hopefully, he would get to resolve the problem tonight because there was a problem. He was absolutely sure of it.

Ruby's grades had taken a jump off the cliff, and final exams were only weeks away.

He wouldn't sit back and watch one of his most promising students self-destruct.

His chest tightened, and his fingers twitched as he edged towards desperation.

What was wrong with him? How could a woman ten years younger than him turn him into such a mess that he would be driven to rash actions?

Still, here he was waiting in anticipation for her arrival.

He sucked in a deep breath, held it for a count of five, and puffed it out again.

Once he'd steadied himself, he relaxed back into his seat only for his heart to pick up speed as Ruby entered the lounge and sashayed in his direction with poise and confidence.

She was dressed in the usual uniform with hair tied back and black ballet pumps on her feet. She stopped the other end of the side table and pulled out a small notepad, pen in hand.

Her eyes had dark circles, and she stared straight ahead, not blinking much, not smiling. "Good evening, sir. What can I get you?"

She seemed to have lost some of her fire and defiance.

Still, she stood with poise, an African queen who had just granted him an audience, a beautiful sight to behold.

Warmth radiated through him, and he felt rejuvenated. Some of his worries vanished.

"Good evening, Ruby. How are you?" he said in a light tone as he beamed a smile at her.

Her eyes widened in surprise as she looked at him, and then they narrowed in suspicion. "I'm ... okay, sir."

"Don't look so worried. I'm not going to make you do anything you don't want."

She exhaled, relaxing her shoulders. "Okay."

"I'd like to discuss something with you if you don't mind," he said.

She shifted from one foot to the other. "My shift ends in a few minutes."

He leaned into his chair. "When your shift ends, we can talk, if you'd rather clock out first."

She kept her gaze averted. "No, I don't. I have a date."

He flinched as if she'd slapped him and blurted out in surprise, "A date?"

She was dating? Of course, she would date.

After all, he'd been seeing other women until two months ago.

Until he couldn't get the image of Ruby prone across his lap out of his mind.

"Yes, a date." She shifted again and lifted her pad and pen. "Do you want me to get you a drink before I go?"

"No." There was no mistaking the order.

She stiffened. "Okay."

Damn it. No coercion, remember?

Still, he couldn't let her go. Not yet. Not until he'd solved the mystery of her declining academic standards.

He gentled his voice. "Postpone your date."

He wanted her to cancel it altogether. But he'd settle for a compromise.

"Why should I?" She tilted her chin, the fire back in her gaze.

That's my girl. His soul cheered at the challenge in her voice.

He'd missed the passion she exuded during her debates in class.

"We need to talk," he said, matter of fact.

"You said that already." Her tone was flippant.

"Watch your tone, young lady," he warned.

"Or what? You'll spank me?" She held his gaze, daring him without fear to step up and take charge of the situation, of her.

He wouldn't disappoint her. "Yes, I will."

Her eyes widened, and she blinked several times. Then, she lowered her gaze. "I'm sorry, sir."

The air around them seemed to crackle as the dynamic between them shifted in a positive direction for the first time in months.

"Apology accepted," he said.

"Thank you, sir."

A sizzle went down his spine at the softness of her voice.

"Look at me, Ruby." He wanted her to see that he meant no harm.

She lifted her head, her beautiful almond-shaped eyes filled with curiosity shadowed by sorrow.

"Will you stay and chat with me, please?" He could charm when he wanted to do so.

She didn't say anything for a few heart-thumping seconds before she tilted her lips upwards. "I'll stay."

"Good. First, please bring me a bottle of Coke, and you can take a drink for yourself, on my tab, of course. When you come back, please take a seat in the chair."

"Yes, sir. I'll be right back."

His heart danced as she walked away, and he had to stop himself from thrusting a fist skyward. But the grin stayed on his face until she returned with two Coca-Cola bottles and glasses.

She placed his on the small table beside his chair before doing the same with hers. Then, she sat in the other armchair at a right angle to his.

He poured his drink into the glass and waited for her to do the same. Then, he lifted the glass. "Salut."

"Cheers," she said.

He took a sip of the cola, and they sat in silence, the music not loud enough to intrude.

She didn't try to speak, which made him happy. She seemed content to let him lead.

After a minute or so, he said, "You missed the lecture this week. Why?"

She grimaced and didn't meet his gaze. "I went to a protest march."

He twisted, not believing what he'd heard. "You ruined your one hundred per cent attendance record because of a demonstration?"

"We demonstrated to get Justice for Darfur against the Sudanese government that refused to hand over to the ICC the war criminals responsible for the persecutions, rapes, and murders of civilians in West Darfur villages. It's a good cause."

She turned to him, face and body animated. The first time he'd seen her passionate about any topic in months. This was the Ruby he missed in class.

Instead of directing her passion to the debates in the school, she missed lectures and joined a protest rally. Dangerous. He couldn't condone her actions.

"I'm aware of the ongoing conflict in the Darfur region and the human rights atrocities allegedly committed by certain individuals—"

"Allegedly?" she interrupted him and jabbed her left arm in the air. "The named men have systematically killed Darfuri men, women, and children. They are committing genocide, for goodness' sake."

"Regardless." He sharpened his tone as a warning. "As a future lawyer, you should know that until they have their day in court and are found guilty, the accusations are just allegations."

"I know. That's why we want the Sudanese government to hand them over to the International Criminal Court at The Hague so that they can stand trial. I was doing the right thing."

He puffed out an exasperated breath. "You may have had the right intentions, but you did the wrong thing—"

"I didn't." She shook her head, watching him.

It was almost as if she was pushing the boundaries and testing the limits of what she was allowed to do.

He leaned back into his chair, picked his drink, and took a sip. He allowed the quietness between them to stretch so she could reflect on her words and actions. Other sounds from the venue intruded—conversations, laughter, and music.

She shifted in her seat and fiddled with her glass but didn't drink from it.

After a minute, he spoke. "Ruby, are you ready to listen?"

She drew in a long breath and puffed it out. "Yes. I'm sorry for interrupting you."

He nodded. "I'll let it pass this time. My concern is for your wellbeing. At the start of this year, you were on track for a First Class Honours. Now, your work standards have dropped. You're late to class. You don't participate. And you think skipping class altogether is a good idea. What is going on with you, Ruby?"

She glanced at him and lowered her gaze.

He didn't miss the shimmer of tears in her eyes. His chest tightened, and his fingers itched to reach out and touch her. Soothe her.

Still, he needed to give her room to express herself or not.

"I'm not doing great," she said in a croaky voice. "I just want this school year to end already so I can go home."

The melancholy in her voice twisted his gut. "Why? What's wrong?"

She shrugged again. "I ..."

"It's okay. You can tell me. I won't judge. I just know there's something wrong, and I want to help."

"I'm sorry, sir. I just ..." She puffed out a breath. "I fell in love with a guy. I thought there was going to be something between us. But he's not interested. It's hard to see him sometimes when I know he's with other women."

His heart twisted that she was in love with someone else. Probably another student. He wanted to find the guy and crush him.

He yearned to pull her into his arms and tell her that he had more love to offer than a thousand young men could give her.

What the hell?

When did this become about love?

It wasn't that he couldn't love her, although he shouldn't.

It was just that he didn't have time for love.

He was a busy man with goals and ambitions. He didn't have time for commitment.

This was the reason he settled for the Bar Atlantic encounters—brief, swift, and pleasurable with no strings attached.

A girl like her came with strings.

Strings that would bind them for a lifetime.

He should just enjoy her company for these few minutes and move right along.

He should send her back downstairs.

Instead, he reached across and cupped her cheek, stroking his thumb down the soft skin. "I'm sorry for your heartache, M'orae. But you shouldn't waste your heart on a guy who can't fall in love with a creature as beautiful and intelligent as you."

For the first time in weeks, months, she smiled at him, her tawny eyes catching the light as her lips bowed sensually. Her long black lashes fluttered against the flawless copper-hued skin.

She was such a gorgeous creature.

All his yearning for her returned and hit him with the force of one of those new high-speed trains, leaving him breathless.

"Thank you," she said in a low voice.

He had to strain to hear the words.

"You're welcome." He withdrew his hand and picked up his drink again. "I need you to make me a promise."

"Oh." She sat up, turning her body in his direction. "What is it?"

"Hello, Zain," a female voice called out. He glanced up as Karidja approached. "It's good to see you again. May I join you?"

"I'll leave you to it," Ruby muttered in a sharp tone as she stood.

Zain grabbed her arm, preventing her from walking away. "There's no need for you to leave. Sit, please."

She stared from him to Kari and back again before she returned to the chair, her lips in a tight line.

He tilted his head to look at the new arrival. "Hello, Kari. It's good to see you again, too. But I was having a conversation with Ruby, so perhaps another time."

Kari's jaw tightened. She didn't look pleased. Still, she plastered a smile on her face and said, "Of course. Catch you later."

She swivelled and walked away.

He loosened his grip on Ruby's arm and twirled his thumb around her wrist.

Underneath, her pulse thumped fast and hard. Her breath caught, but she didn't lift her head.

"Ruby, look at me."

She turned slowly, and her chin jutted out, her eyes glaring.

"I'm sorry about the interruption," he said in a placating tone.

Kari shouldn't have tried to insinuate herself into their discussion. And it seemed Ruby didn't like the woman anyway, considering her behaviour the last time.

"Your apology is accepted," she pronounced with the haughtiness of a queen.

He hid his smile. She was adorable. He wanted to build a palace for her and give her a kingdom.

"Good. But next time, don't get up from your seat unless I give you permission."

"Or what? You'll spank me?" Her eyes held no fear, only challenged him.

This was the second time tonight she'd mentioned the punishment.

His heart thumped hard. Did she want his hands on her body, coaxing her into submission?

He nodded. "That's one of the possibilities if we were lovers."

He wouldn't discipline someone he had no interest it.

Here, it was a prelude to more, a kind of foreplay, as long as all parties involved were willing.

"Oh." Her eyes widened, riveted to him as she tucked the corner of her bottom lip between her teeth. "So my disobedience is an invitation for you to take it further?"

He continued stroking her wrist, her pulse beating fast against his thumb. "I told you before, naughty girls get punished. Is that what you're doing, Ruby? Are you misbehaving because you want my attention?"

Her throat rippled as she swallowed, and then, she shrugged. "You wanted me to make a promise. What was it?"

He allowed the change of topic. In any case, he'd come here because of his worry about her school work. Nothing more.

Liar.

He released her arm and relaxed again.

"Firstly, you will not miss any more lectures, and I'm not talking about mine alone. I will check your attendances with the Faculty office." He counted them off on his fingers. "Secondly, you will be punctual, return to sitting in the front row, and participate in my classes. Thirdly, you will not attend any more demonstrations for the rest of the semester. Instead, you will focus your efforts in preparing for the upcoming examinations."

She grimaced as he listed out the items, staring at a point on the floor. Then, she turned to him. "I'm going to make the promise on one condition."

"Name it," he said, curious to know what she'd ask for. He would grant her the world if he could.

"Promise me that you will not have sex with Kari or anyone else anymore." She made a strong demand, didn't flinch or hesitate.

"You can't ask me to do that." His denial was driven by shock more than anything else.

He could harp on about being her lecturer, about ethics and morals, about rules and regulations.

Then again, he'd blurred the lines a long time ago. She'd said nothing he hadn't already thought.

She stiffened and glared at him. "Can't I? You told me I was beautiful and intelligent just minutes ago. Was that a lie?"

"Of course not." His forehead furrowed in a frown. He would never lie to her.

"You look at me as if I am the most fascinating thing on the planet." She stabbed her chest with her thumb. "I think you're sexy and smart and one of the best lecturers I have. I know wanting you is wrong, but I can't stop."

She wanted him?

She wanted him.

His heart soared, his skin warming. Not to mention his suddenly tight trousers, strangling his blooming cock.

She paused, staring at him as if she tried to read him.

He kept his expression schooled although he wanted to pull her up and take her for a spin around the dance floor. He should kiss her and spank her and love her.

She huffed out air, pushed off the chair, and stood. "If you're going to pretend there's nothing between us, that's your headache, but I'm done."

"I warned you not to do that." A surge of adrenaline went through him as he grabbed her arm, tugged her back, and upended her over his lap.

Her head and arms were on the floor while her hips and legs dangled from his lap over the other side.

"What—"

Her protest cut off as soon as he brought his hand down on her bum in hard swats. She didn't fight or struggle. Her body stayed limp, only jolting with the impacts of his palm on her yielding flesh, through the fabric of her skirt.

He didn't stop until he got to ten, his palm tingling.

Nobody intervened. After the initial curiosity by the other guests, they went back to their previous activities. Even the service employees ignored him.

"You can stand up now," he said when he finished.

Slowly, she pushed off and swayed as she stood, looking spaced out.

"Ruby, sit on my lap," he ordered.

She lowered her body on his thighs, winced, and then shifted as she tried to get comfortable.

He wrapped his left hand around her body, letting her soft curves settle on him. "Do you understand what just happened?"

He'd just staked his claim on her, and he wanted to be sure they were on the same page.

She nodded and tucked her face into his shoulder.

"I want words." He insisted and tugged her so he could see her expression.

She looked everywhere but at him. "I ... I ..."

Large drops spilt from her eyes as she trembled with quiet sobs.

He tugged her head back onto his shoulders and stroked his hands down her back.

"That's okay ... Let it all out ... Tears are good."

"It's just," she spoke between sobs. "The past few months have been tough. I felt so stressed out."

"I know. I'm here," he said in a soft voice as he continued caressing her skin. "You're mine, now. I won't let you suffer again."

"Do you promise?" she sniffed into his shirt.

"I promise." He didn't hesitate.

He put his life and his career on the line for her. If anyone ever found out, he would lose his tenure, no doubt, even though this was the first time he'd held her.

He needed her, and she seemed to need him in return.

He was done watching her from a distance.

Her body stopped trembling, and after a few inhalations, she calmed.

He dug out his handkerchief and handed it to her, and she wiped her face.

He cupped her cheek. "Are you feeling better now?"

"Yes, thanks."

"You're welcome, M'orae."

"Good evening, Zain. Is everything alright here?"

Zain glanced up.

The owner of Bar Atlantic looked at them with enquiring eyes, hands in his trouser pockets. Kehinde 'Kenny' Cruz was an old friend. They had met a long time ago as law students before Kenny had joined the Nigerian Armed Forces like the rest of his military-orientated family. But he'd resigned his commission a few years ago, moved to London, and set up this club.

The man knew Zain well enough that he would never overstep his boundaries at the club. But it was a member of his staff sitting on Zain's lap, so he was entitled to ask questions.

"Hello, Kenny. Yes, everything is wonderful. I was just taking care of my precious here. Ruby, please let Kenny know how you're feeling. Don't be afraid. Just tell him the truth."

She lifted her head, blinking slowly. "I'm feeling good, Mister K. Just a little wobbly, that's all."

"Good. Do you need anything?" Kenny said.

"Please get her a glass of water," Zain said. "Also, I'd like to take her home. So if someone can bring her items, I'd be grateful."

"It's not a problem. I'll get that sorted for you. It was nice seeing you again, Zain. We must catch up soon."

"Sure. We'll do that, Kenny."

The man gave them one last look before striding away.

A waiter brought a glass of water, and Zain thanked him before giving it to Ruby. She emptied the glass but didn't attempt to get up from his lap.

"Good evening, sir. I brought Ruby's stuff." A waitress arrived with her coat and tote.

Ruby lifted her head. "Amara."

"Are you okay?" Amara asked as she glanced for her to him.

"Yes, I'm okay. Thanks for bringing my stuff." She shifted. "Sir, can I get up now?"

"Sure." He let her go although he wanted to hold onto her for a few more moments. But that would have to wait. "Are you going to introduce me to your friend?"

"Yes. Of course. This is my friend. Amara, this is Mister Zain."

"It's nice to meet you, sir," the girl said.

"It's nice to meet you, too, Amara. Thanks for bringing her bag." He stood, too. "I'm going to pay my tab, and then, we'll head out shortly."

He wanted to give them a chance to talk and also give Ruby the option of changing her mind. The experience of the last few minutes must be overwhelming for her.

He left them and strode over to the bar where Kenny stood chatting to the manager.

"I'd like my bill," he said to the barman before turning to Kenny. "I'm sorry to drag one of your staff away."

He hadn't planned for the evening to progress in this direction. But he had no regrets.

Kenny grinned at him. "For the past few weeks, you turn up and just sit in a chair staring at her like a lovesick lion that isn't sure if he wants to maul the goat or take it home as a pet. I'm glad you finally made up your mind."

Zain chuckled as he slotted his card into the machine and tapped his pin on the pad. "Trust you to hit the nail right on the head."

He had been acting forlorn the past weeks. He just hadn't thought anyone had noticed.

"How did you know I was watching her?" he asked as he glanced at Ruby who was still chatting with her friend. He put his card back in his wallet along with the receipt. "You have other staff working on that floor."

"When she asked to change floors, I suspected something was up and told the manager to keep an eye on her. And then, after her interaction with you that one week, she asked to be reassigned back downstairs. And then you show up, and you don't mingle with the other guests and spend your time watching through the glass. That could only mean one thing."

"And what's that?"

"You have it bad for her."

Zain scratched his chin and grinned. "I do."

"So which one did you decide? Are you mauling her or keeping her?"

He pushed away from the bar. "That, my friend, would be telling. See you another time."

"Take care." They embraced before he headed back to his chair.

"I'll see you at home, Amara." Ruby shrugged on her coat and picked up her bag.

"See you later," her friend said before returning to her duties.

He took Ruby's hand. "Are you sure about this? You can change your mind, and we can forget tonight ever happened."

She shook her head as she held his gaze. "I'm not changing my mind. Tonight is the best thing that has happened to me in months. I don't want to forget about it. I want to be with you. You promised you wouldn't let me suffer again. Were you telling a lie?"

"No. I will never lie to you. I keep my promises." He pushed a stray curl of hair behind her ear and stroked the lobe. Her breath hitched. His lips curled into a smile at her responsiveness. "Being with me means you also have to keep some promises. Are you going to adhere to the items I listed?"

She tilted her head to the side and smiled shyly. "I'll be good. I promise I'll do everything you mentioned. But ..." She bit the corner of her lower lip.

He tilted her chin up. "What is it?"

"What about Kari?"

"You shouldn't worry about her. I haven't been with her or anyone else in months."

Her eyes glittered in the low light as her lips curled in a slow smile. "Are you serious?"

He lowered his hand and slapped her bum. "Do you doubt me?"

"Ouch." She winced. "No."

"That's good." He grinned as he placed his arm around her shoulders and guided her towards the exit.

She tucked her body into him, her arm going around his back as they headed down the stair and did the short walk to the underground car park.

Then, he opened the door for her and waited for her to settle before shutting the door and walking over to the other side.

And as he drove out of the car park, he glanced at her smiling face.

For the first time, he'd given in to a whim. His life would never be the same again.

PART TWO

AT WAR

CHAPTER SIX

GANURI REGION, WANAI
FEBRUARY 2017

"NOT again."

Zain strode along the dusty unpaved road, his limbs heavy and muscles stiff as he surveyed the devastation.

Armed guards—his men—scouted along the edge of the road, checking the houses for survivors.

Most of them lay empty, the occupants having fled.

He hoped most had escaped the massacre.

Blood, from those who hadn't evaded the marauders, stained the scorched terracotta earth in dark patches underneath the strewn bodies he and his men stumbled upon in their search.

The eerie silence was a deafening clang only broken by the occasional outcry when one of his team found a survivor in this chaos.

Sometimes, a small whirlpool of dust would roll only to flatten as if Nature, too, had lost hope. The sun glared down, making his skin and shirt damp from the perspiration.

"Here!" Samuel, one of his adoptive brothers, called out. "It's a boy. He's alive."

Zain ran. A member of the medical team who had responded to his request for emergency services raced on ahead.

He reached Samuel as he dragged a child who'd been buried underneath two unmoving bodies out of the gutter. The partially-covered drain ran along the side of the road.

"The others?" Zain stopped in front of a shop with a sign that read 'Yara Fashion.'

"Dead. Gunshots." Samuel indicated the adult female body still in the drain and placed the child on the smooth concrete veranda of the closed shop.

Zain's stomach rolled with nausea, and he fought to retain his composure. This wasn't the place or time to give in to the emotions threatening to overwhelm him. He needed to focus on saving as many people as possible.

The child trembled, his breath coming out in gasps as he muttered and cried. His body was covered in dirt and blood, making it difficult to see if he had any physical injuries.

"Clean him up and check him over," Aliyah, another adoptive sibling, called out from where she attended to someone who lay on a different concrete terrace. She led the medical team whose job was to determine the degree of urgency for each case.

Zain had seen her group in action enough times to have a rough idea of how things worked.

The dead or dying were at the bottom of the list. The injured were prioritised based on those who needed immediate help and those who could wait.

They would be transported to the nearest hospital, which was about sixteen kilometres away in Boma.

"Get some water," he shouted as he squatted in front of the boy who couldn't be more than ten years old, from his size.

Someone jogged to one of the trucks and grabbed a bottle from the stack they had brought along.

"Don't be afraid. My name is Zain. What's your name?" he asked in the local language, keeping his tone gentle so as not to frighten the boy.

The child kept his gaze riveted on Zain. "Ifeh."

"Ifeh, are you hurt anywhere?" He wiped the boy's face with his handkerchief. The smudges seemed to be dirt, not blood.

The kid shook his head and coughed.

"Here's the water," someone said behind Zain.

He didn't look up, just moved his hand, so the bottle was placed on his palm. He unscrewed and tilted it.

Ifeh gulped down half of the drink before shoving the bottle in Zain's direction.

"You can keep it in case you need more."

"Thank you," Ifeh replied, clutching the plastic container to his chest. "I know who you are."

"What do you mean?" Zain asked.

"You are The Professor. Papa talked about you."

"Yes, I am." Zain smiled. Few in this region didn't know of him even if they'd never seen him. "Can you tell us what happened here?"

The boy swallowed, and his body shook. "I was playing with my friends on the street when the men arrived in trucks. They were the bad men Mama talked about with her friends when she thought I was not listening. They were carrying guns and started shooting people. I told my friends to hide, and I ran as fast as I could until I saw Mama. She pushed me in the gutter to hide. She said I should stay quiet. I went in. But before she could hide with me, they shot her, and she fell on top of me. They killed Mama."

Ifeh sobbed.

Zain pulled the crying child into his arms and hugged him. His heart broke for the kid and the many others who had lost loved ones.

When the boy calmed down and had been cleared by the medical team, Zain handed him over to another member of his team who would take him to the local primary school where they had the emergency relief base.

By the time they'd completed the search and counted the bodies, the death toll reached twenty-four from gunshots and machete cuts. Many of the town's people had run away and hidden in the bushes to avoid the massacre.

Some of them started returning when word got around that it was safe to do so.

The local police showed up about two hours after the attack, and the military eventually turned up, four hours after them. Even the state governor showed up.

Zain spent over an hour in a meeting with the governor, police inspector, and army unit commander who seemed all talk and bluster and no substance.

"Why did it take you two hours to respond to this attack?" he asked the chief of police after he had briefed them on what his emergency crew had completed before their arrivals.

The man moved uncomfortably in his seat. "Unfortunately, my men don't have the firepower to deal with this kind of attack. We called the military as soon as we got news."

Zain wasn't surprised that the man passed the buck to the other security officer.

All eyes shifted to the army commander who stared at them for a few ticks before saying, "We got here as soon as we could. It wasn't as if we had any prior knowledge of this attack."

"How can you not have any prior knowledge? What is the job of military intelligence or the police, for that matter?" Zain could not contain his dissatisfaction at the way law enforcement had handled these attacks so far.

The army man stiffened. "We are doing our best."

"Your best is not good enough," he said, pissed off by their attitudes. He was usually more diplomatic, but that ship had sailed.

This was the fifth attack in the past year. And neither the military nor the police force had made any progress with arresting the group terrorising the people of Ganuri.

"What right do you have to talk to me like that?" the man preened.

"I have every right as a citizen of Wanai. As soon as I got news of the attack, I got into my car and drove out here. My team were first on the scene. We didn't know what we would face, but we still came here."

"How do we know that you and your team didn't orchestrate the attack in the first place?"

Zain's blood boiled, and he shoved his chair back, tipping it over. He gripped the table as he leaned in the direction of the military guy. "You think I did this? You think the MLG ... that we would murder our own people? For what purposes exactly?"

"Gentlemen, please calm down," the governor intervened. "I'd like to talk to Mr. Bassong alone."

After a few tense seconds, the army commander and police inspector walked out.

Zain paced up and down before righting his chair and settling into it.

"You don't believe the nonsense about the MLG being involved with these attacks, do you?" he asked.

The governor was one of the administrators in the Ganuri region. His citizens had been massacred today.

"You know I don't believe that nonsense," the man said quietly. "But I'm going to be honest with you. I just came back from a meeting of the governors and the president yesterday. President Doona is officially naming the MLG as a terrorist organisation. He says that your quest to split Wanai and create a nation of Ganuri is nothing more than terrorism, and he has put the blame of these recent attacks squarely on your shoulders as the leader of the MLG."

Zain's blood ran cold.

What the fuck?

No wonder the arrogant army commander had blatantly accused him of engineering the attack. He'd thought the man was just trying to hide his incompetence.

But something more sinister could be going on.

"Do you think I'm responsible for the attacks?"

"No. I don't. But even if it's not your orders, it will be labelled as a breakaway faction of the MLG who want to start a civil war or something."

This was getting more ridiculous by the second.

"A breakaway faction. There is no such thing. The MLG is a political organisation. We have no military affiliation."

The governor shrugged. "It doesn't matter. Doona wants you to drop this quest for Ganuri Independence, and he will do it by any means necessary."

Zain read between the lines.

"What are you saying? Were the attacks ordered by Doona?"

"I didn't say that. All I'm saying is that no matter who is orchestrating the attacks, you are going to get the blame. And in the meantime, more of Ganuri's citizens will suffer. You don't want that, surely?"

The shock of that news stayed with him for hours until he returned to his home in Boma. When he walked into his private residence, the hands of the wall clock read one-thirty-five in the morning.

Exhaustion weighed down his body. However, sleep remained the last thing on his mind. He couldn't snooze peacefully after what he had witnessed today.

That had been the fifth spate of unprovoked attacks targeting villages and towns in the Ganuri region over the past year. On each occasion, innocent lives had been lost, and the military and government had done nothing to protect the citizens by catching the culprits.

Many people from the villages and towns had not returned to their homes for fear of more onslaughts. There were currently over fifty thousand internally displaced people in the region living in camps.

Letting out a sigh, he stripped off his clothes and walked into the bathroom for a shower.

He caught his reflection in the mirror above the sink.

Memories he'd locked away assaulted him—a dark, dank room, a snarling face, and excruciating pain—replaying how he'd acquired the scars on his chest that felt like marks on his soul.

His chest tightened, and he became disorientated. His body jerked, and he gripped the sink with clammy hands to stop from toppling over as he relived the torture.

These vivid flashbacks seemed to be triggered whenever he came across violent devastation like he'd seen earlier, opening up the floodgates of emotions sown nine years ago.

Those carefree days when he'd lived in London, and his biggest hassle had been marking law papers for undergraduates, had vanished as if they'd never existed.

One undergraduate had changed everything.

Fuelled by rage, he overcame the dizzy spell and pushed away from the sink, banishing the memories.

He wouldn't rehash the past. His focus would remain on the future of the people of Ganuri.

Turning on the faucet, he stepped under the spray. Cold water stung his skin, invigorating him.

In a few minutes, he would chair an impromptu meeting with his team. He needed a clear head.

Ten minutes later, dressed in a long flowing white cotton jalabia, he strode into his living room to find Solomon, Samuel, and Latifah already seated.

Samuel and Solomon were twins born to his mother's friend who had been killed during the Sierra Leonean war. The boys had been abducted and converted to child soldiers. His mother had worked for years first to find them, and then to rehabilitate them from the trauma they had endured. She had adopted and raised them.

Latifah was his cousin, the daughter of his mother's brother. She was older than him and had worked for military intelligence. Sometimes, they teased her and called her Jane Bond, to which she would reply, "No. I'm Jill Reacher."

These were his three most trusted allies, aside from his mother and Aliyah. Of course, they were family, too, so the bond stayed strong.

An assortment of snacks was laid out on the coffee table, the first thing they would eat since they'd gotten news of the siege.

He settled on a sofa and stretched out his legs.

"Tell me we're going to do something about this new development." Samuel was first off the mark.

He'd briefed them about his conversation with the governor on the way home.

"We are," Zain replied. "I want you to find out the cost of setting up secure zones in every major town in Ganuri as well as the cost of training and equipping the vigilante teams who are going to operate them. If the government is not going to protect the people, then we will."

"We're not a military outfit," Solomon spoke.

"We're not. This is not war."

"Yet," Latifah interjected.

"That's right. Not yet. We're going to do what the police and the civil defence corps are supposed to do. Under the Wanaian constitution, the citizens have the right to defend their lives, loved ones, and properties against unknown assailants. This is why we need to create safe zones because we can defend those who come to us for shelter. What we can't do is be on the offensive."

"But they are blaming us for the attacks. Won't this make it worse?" Solomon asked.

"Not in my opinion," Samuel said. "They are going to blame us, whatever happens. At least this way, we will protect the people and hopefully reduce the loss of lives and property."

"I agree," said Latifah. "By calling us terrorists, Doona is declaring war on the people of Ganuri. I think we will be foolish if we don't show him that we can match his force."

Zain scrubbed a hand over his face. "We are in a difficult situation. This wasn't the plan for the MLG, but since we have been shoved into the corner, we have to respond. But before we actually finalise everything, I want everyone to get some sleep. If we are still in agreement in the light of day, then we will get started."

"Good," Samuel said.

Solomon nodded.

"There's something you need to see first." Latifah pulled her phone from her pocket and tapped on the screen before pushing it across the table.

"What is it?" Zain leaned over to see the screen. The volume was loud enough for everyone to hear. It seemed to be a clip from a television broadcast.

"It's been in the news." Her eyes were blazing, her hands balled into fists. "The day that tens of people are slaughtered, our president holds a party to announce the engagement of his son."

The screen showed a newsreel of the president and his family and then switched to the president's son with a woman.

Blood drained from Zain's head.

He registered Latifah's angry words, but it was the young woman standing next to Kweku Doona that had his mind reeling.

Princess Isha Saene.

The flashback returned, and he travelled to the gloomy cell. Rattling chains bound him to the wall, cold sneering laughter rang in his ears, and words he would never forget shredded his heart. *"She is not who you think she is ... She was playing you, fool."*

His skin grew clammy, and his heart raced.

Gripping his head, he fought the images bombarding him.

Slowly, the sounds of his team's conversation filtered into his mind.

"But that's not the worst thing of all." Latifah's voice was firm. "Do you realise what that marriage means? King Ibrahim Saene is one of the most respected and most powerful African leaders, certainly in West Africa."

"His daughter's marriage to Doona's son will mean that Doona has the backing of one of the most powerful nations in Africa, which means he gets a license to behave any way he likes," Solomon added.

"Kind of like France backing Cameroon while it commits human rights violations against the regional separatists," Samuel said.

"Zain?" Latifah called out.

He lifted his head. Everyone's gaze was on him.

"Are you okay? Did you hear what we said?" Latifah continued.

"Yes, I heard you." His mouth seemed filled with sawdust. He scrubbed his palms over his face and puffed out a breath. "The Ganuri people will not get their freedom if Doona marries the Saene princess."

"And our people will continue to be killed without recourse for justice. We can't let that continue," Latifah said. "I have a plan."

Chapter Seven

Lagos, Nigeria

March 2018

"I CAN'T believe you finally said yes to marriage."

Isha gulped hard, and her throat hurt. She swallowed her drink with difficulty at the mention of the 'm' word.

"I did. So?" she replied with a blasé lift of shoulders. Feigning nonchalance at her friend's teasing but true words, she tipped the liquid content of the flute into her mouth.

The sharp flavour of champagne—almonds, orange zest, and white cherry—bubbled on her tongue, washing the sour dread away.

Wedlock had been an impending certainty from the moment she'd become an adult.

As the eldest daughter of King Ibrahim Saene, sovereign ruler of the Kingdom of Bagumi, royal blood flowed in her veins. She was a proud member of the Royal House of Saene, loyal to her lineage, and duty-bound to her country.

Through the centuries, her regal ancestors had maintained their dominance in the region through matrimonial alliances with other powerful nations, each prince or princess matched with a counterpart from a neighbouring kingdom.

Those traditions remained significant, even in this century.

As the First Princess, everyone expected her to comply and select a dignified suitor from a pre-approved list of noble candidates.

After years of postponing the inevitable and focusing on her career as a lawyer and corporate negotiator, she had accepted a wedding proposal. Options had once again been put before her, and this time, she had chosen.

Now, was it the *right* choice— No, she refused to think of that. Not now. Not tonight.

In celebration of her upcoming nuptials, her friends Amara and Joya had organised this pre-bachelorette event in Lagos. Her weeklong business trip to Nigeria had been extended to include the weekend of partying.

Her fiancé was on his way and should be arriving soon.

The ballroom of an exclusive hotel overlooking the Atlantic Ocean glittered. Most of Lagos' high society—including the First Lady of the State—gravitated in her direction to extend their good wishes.

Cold air blasted from the air conditioners, swirling around her bare shoulders and down her body covered in crimson silk and chiffon from bodice to toes.

The vast, open windows showed the spotlighted, green grassy vista of the lawn, the starry cobalt skies, and indigo waves crashing against white sands.

Amara shifted forward in her gold and burgundy padded seat. One of Isha's oldest friends, she looked beatific in the sugar-cookie-coloured satin dress contrasting against her flawless chocolate skin.

She lifted Isha's hand with soft, slender digits. "People will kill for these rocks."

Light refracted off the massive diamond ring on her finger, scattering prisms and rainbows across her vision. The oval-shaped stone at the centre of the intricately designed and breath-taking platinum ring was flanked by dazzling trapezoid diamonds and surrounded by a brilliant pavé halo.

"Kweku is sparing no expense," Joya, another friend and later addition to the group, said. She wore an ivory halter-neck wide-leg jumpsuit, blending with the colour theme.

Her friends had insisted on a strict dress code for invitees. As the celebrant, Isha wore red, which happened to be her favourite colour, while every other attendee had dressed in various shades of cream.

"I wish he would spare the expense," Isha replied with a grimace.

As the son of the Head of State of Wanai, Kweku Doona had the position equivalent to Crown Prince and had recently been announced as his father's successor. He proclaimed his prestige in the luxurious items he owned, from fast cars to racehorses. In the years that they had courted, he had taken her on trips around the world from Monte Carlo to New York. There would be no doubt that he could keep her in the lap of luxury, although she had her own immense income.

She had never been naturally lavish, much to her mother's chagrin. The older woman always referred to the various charities founded by the family, as if that created a balance for the extravagant royal lifestyle. She subscribed to the Chinese proverb, which said, "Teach a man to fish, and he will feed himself for a lifetime."

As a patron to a foundation that sponsored various education and works programmes, Isha preferred to sink her personal income into projects that supported the less privileged than splash out on gaudy jewellery.

However, being a princess came with certain perks she couldn't avoid.

"Anyone who sees this ring will know how much he values you above all else." Amara released Isha's fingers as she leaned into the seat.

"Really?" She tilted her head, brows raised as she suppressed laughter.

Her friend was sarcastic, surely. Amara remained unlikely to be swayed by expensive items since her family was one of the richest on the continent. Like Isha, she had never been driven by the urge to flaunt her wealth, which made them such great pals.

"Yes, the bigger the ring, the better." Amusement laced Amara's words. She lifted her flute in salutation.

Isha played along with the joke. She angled her hand as if examining the sparkling jewellery. "By your words, then, this ring guarantees me a happy marriage?"

"If I had that ring on my finger, I'd be happy." Joya's giggle tinkled like merry bells.

"Be serious."

"I am."

Their chuckles proved the opposite.

"Okay. Okay," Amara conceded. "The ring doesn't guarantee your happiness. But at least, it shows he cares enough to go to all that expense."

"And on top of that," Joya chimed in. "The two of you are the hottest couple in Africa at the moment. You, the daughter of a King, and him, the son of a president, and you've been dating for years. Surely, it's a match made in Heaven. You must both be in love."

The heavy burden resettled on Isha's chest. She struggled to breathe.

She had once been in love.

A long time ago.

A lifetime ago.

She had been barely out of her teen years when she'd fallen in heedless love at university. She'd given her heart without reservations. Until her lover had deserted her and left her heart in tatters.

Devastated, she'd vowed never to give her heart to another man. She'd refocused her energies on building her career as a lawyer and performing her royal duties as a princess.

She wouldn't be foolish enough to repeat the reckless error of her youth.

Consequently, her agreement to marry Kweku proved to be a matter of the head, not the heart. The palace matchmaker had provided a shortlist of suitors. Out of the men she had dated, Kweku had proved the most determined. He accepted her desire to carve out a life and had been patient enough despite her reluctance to tie the knot at earlier opportunities.

They enjoyed each other's company and held mutual respect and perhaps some affection.

Nothing like the all-consuming passion of the past.

Passion didn't make for a successful union.

Commitment and compassion would be the key.

And she had both in abundance.

"Kweku is a good man, and we'll be happy together." She hoped.

Marriages in her social circles were matches made to secure strategic alliances between nations. It had worked for her father. No reason it shouldn't work for her.

"You will be." Joya patted her hand in affirmation.

"I concur," Amara joined in.

They raised the champagne flutes and converged in a toast. The clinking glasses mixed with the sound of the live band playing Afro Jazz.

Isha leaned into her seat and took another sip of the bubbly drink. Closing her eyes, she allowed her body to relax.

"I read some news online the other day about Wanai."

Her lashes fluttered open. "What was it?"

"There's a province of Wanai looking to break away and form a new nation. It caught my attention because of you and Kweku. Do you know what's going on there? There seems to be a media blackout. I read that they're not allowing journalists into the region."

Her spine stiffened. A journalist had asked her a similar question a few days ago. She'd been annoyed because the media focus of her trip had been diverted from the pan-African trade deal she had negotiated for her Kingdom to events in Wanai which were outside of her control and jurisdiction.

Then, she had given astute comments to the journalists, knowing her words would reflect on Kweku.

Now, she wouldn't hide her true feelings about the situation. There was no need for tactfulness amongst close friends.

"Don't get me started. No one seems to understand how difficult it is to rule a country of multiple tribes. Kweku's father has kept Wanai together for years. Now the horrible militants are terrorising the people."

A muffled cough interrupted her diatribe. She glanced up. In her fury, she hadn't noticed the arrival of the serving girl in a black uniform, dark braided hair tied up in a ponytail.

"Would you like more champagne?" the girl asked as she lifted the magnum of Krug Vintage.

"Sure," Joya replied as Isha nodded.

The waitress filled their gilded flutes with the pale-gold liquid before walking away.

"Excuse me, Princess." Her bodyguard, who stood behind her chair, leaned over to speak in a low voice.

The entourage proved to be another absolute necessity she had grown to appreciate over time.

"Yes?" She tilted her head.

"You have a call." He passed a phone over to her. "It's Mr. Doona."

She smiled as she took the muted gadget. "Excuse me, ladies. I need to find a quiet space to take this call."

"Sure."

Her friends waved her on as she got up and sashayed across the lobby, stiletto heels clicking against the marble tiles. Her silent and huge bodyguard kept anyone who wanted to approach at bay while clearing the path to the exit. In the courtyard, she found a quiet corner amongst the trimmed hibiscus hedges. The tide lapped against the concrete barrier, and the sea breeze fluttered the hem of her dress.

"Kweku, where are you?" she asked after pressing the button to connect the call.

"Darling, I'm leaving now." His voice came through along with the sound of activity in the background.

"Just leaving? That means you won't be here for another two hours." She scratched her eyebrow.

"I know. My meeting ran late. But I'll be there soon." He sounded unconcerned.

Isha repressed a sigh. Sometimes, the formal commitments ate into their personal time, another consequence of their statuses. The party would be wrapping up by the time he arrived.

"I told you not to worry about coming over. We can meet up another time. I can do a stopover in Wanai on my way back to Bagumi."

"I haven't seen you in weeks. I'll be there in two hours, and we can spend the weekend together. Got to go."

She puffed out a breath. She couldn't stop him from coming over, even if she didn't see the relevance. With

Kweku, she had found out it was easier to pick some battles and let the rest go. "I'll see you soon."

Puffing out another heavy breath, she lowered the phone and stared at the inky waves only a few meters away. Warm air swirled around her shoulders.

A knot curled tight in her belly, and the sense of unease she'd kept at bay since she'd agreed to marry Kweku seeped into her consciousness.

Why wasn't she overjoyed at her impending nuptials like every other potential bride?

You know why.

The inner voice sounded loud and clear and admonishing.

She shook off the heavy sensation and swivelled. Not the time, nor the place, to go into *that*. Truth be told, it would never be the right moment, and she planned to keep it that way.

Her bodyguard stood a couple of paces away, posture straight and alert.

Something niggled at her. In all the time she'd been dating Kweku, her chief of security had always referred to him in the formal tone as Mr. Doona. While he didn't get overly familiar and chummy with her, he'd never hesitated to speak his mind where her security might be concerned. She'd come to appreciate his candour in this light. There really wasn't anything she couldn't discuss honestly with him.

"Kojo, why do I feel as if you don't like my fiancé?" she asked.

Tall like an iroko tree, built like an armoured tank, and with the agility of a race car, the man had become her symbol of safety in the past few years.

Kojo's face puckered in a frown before it smoothed out. "I have no opinions either way about Mr. Doona."

"I've never known you to be a liar. Why are you doing so now?"

One of the things that made her a great advocate and negotiator was her ability to listen and absorb information from all sides, which ultimately helped her in achieving her goals.

"I'm sorry, My Princess. But it is not my place to share my opinions with you."

"Perhaps not. But can you tell me why you always call him Mr. Doona?"

"Is that not his name?"

"You know exactly what I mean. He is the president's son. You don't seem to have any respect about that."

Kojo stiffened. "Beyond being the president's son, he is nothing else. Just a man."

His tone implied that her fiancé wasn't a good man.

She bristled, although she had given him permission to speak freely. "Do you have the same contempt for me? Do you see me as nothing more than the king's daughter?"

His tone softened. "No, My Princess. You are a princess of Bagumi, a highly placed member of our Royal family. Beyond that, you are a much-esteemed ambassador and an advocate. I see the dedicated way you work tirelessly to improve things in Bagumi. I am very proud of you and honoured to have the position of being your chief bodyguard."

"Thank you, Kojo. However, are you saying that Kweku does not care about his people?"

"I cannot speak for the people of Wanai. I only speak as a Bagumian."

"But?" she prodded, knowing there was more he withheld.

"But, I have heard rumours about things going on in Wanai and in the Ganuri region, especially."

"What kind of rumours?"

"About ethnic cleansing."

Isha's scalp prickled, and she shook her head. She opened her mouth and closed it, her emotions warring.

The idea of people suffering raised the human rights advocate in her to take a stand. Yet, Kweku was the man she had agreed to marry. And neither he nor any members of his family would condone actions that violated their citizens.

"Lies. Just lies. Think about it. If there was ethnic cleansing going on, why isn't it in the news? Why isn't the African Union or the United Nations stepping in? Tell me."

"It could be because there's been a blockade and blackout. The government blocked Internet access for the region, and journalists have been banned from going there."

"That's just to stop fake news being spread on the Internet." That's what Kweku had explained. She believed him. What reason would he have to lie? She would be part of the ruling family of that country, after all—he wouldn't hide such matters from her. "And a journalist got abducted and killed by the Ganuri militants months ago. The government doesn't want to see anyone else dead."

"The rebels say that the government army was responsible for the killing," Kojo interjected.

She had to think as the rational lawyer here, not as an emotional fiancée. "And do you believe the rebels?"

"I don't know. But it seems to me that if the government doesn't want to be accused of maltreating its citizens, it has to be seen to be fair. One way of doing so would be to allow journalists, of course with army protection if necessary, to visit the region and record what is going on. If the rebels are terrorising the locals, then it will become obvious."

The Wanaian government had been trying over the last year to quash the rebels and without much success. Perhaps letting people see the horrors perpetrated by the terrorists would galvanise the rest of the world into helping to end the conflict soon. She would speak to Kweku about it this weekend.

"Thank you, Kojo. I appreciate you speaking your mind with me."

"You're welcome, My Princess," he replied as he held the door for her.

"I will re-join my friends shortly, but first, the ladies' room." She went down the hallway and waited at the threshold while he did a security check of facilities.

He came out and spoke. "All clear."

Low music from hidden speakers piped into the perfumed air. A bouquet of flowers sat in a lilac vase on the shiny black counter.

After using the cubicle, she strode to the middle sink and turned the faucet when the door opened. A uniformed cleaner pushed in a large linen trolley.

"Good evening," the lady said in an accent that wasn't wholly Nigerian.

"'Evening." Isha glanced over as she washed her hands.

The woman was slightly shorter—could be because of Isha's stilettos—and had ebony skin underneath the long black hair with a fringe that almost covered her eyes. She suspected it was a wig and wondered if the length of the hair didn't interfere with the woman's job.

"Let me get that for you." The cleaner pulled out a towel from her stash.

"Thank you." Isha took the warm napkin and dried her hands.

The trolley creaked as the woman pushed it.

Isha assumed she would walk past to continue her duties. Something pricked her neck. "Ow."

Eyes widened, she glanced into the mirror, right hand reaching for the point of pain.

The woman stood behind her, a small syringe in her gloved hand.

The world went hazy. "What did you ... dooo?"

"Go to sleep, Princess."

The woman's words came from a distance as Isha toppled backwards. She landed on a cushion of fluffy warm cotton as more fabric fell on her.

Blackness hovered in her vision.

Opening her mouth, she tried to scream. No sound came out.

She tried to move her limbs. They, too, didn't respond.

She only tumbled further into the abyss.

CHAPTER EIGHT

ZAIN had always seen himself as a virtuous man. A moral man.

But in the past few hours, he had committed several offences. Offences that would see him executed or jailed for life imprisonment at a minimum.

He lived in dire times.

And desperate times called for bold measures.

Even if the consequences of his actions would be his death.

He wasn't afraid to die for what he believed in, though he would rather live to ensure that his people got the future they deserved.

So here he sat in a van marked with the logo of the company that handled the laundry and linen services for the Goldcrest Hotel Suites where a certain princess was celebrating with her friends, oblivious to the unfolding series of actions instigated a year ago.

They had planned this mission over a few short days as soon as one of their spies had informed them of the princess' visit to Lagos. They'd sought opportunities that would deliver her to them. And when they'd heard about plans for the party, it had become the perfect opportunity for them.

Doing something like this would have been more difficult in Wanai since there would have been more security for the future wife of the president's son.

But out here, she travelled like little more than an ordinary citizen, with just one or two bodyguards. They had waylaid the staff of the company providing the laundry service, kept them as prisoners while they carried out this operation. The hotel had become accessible once they'd shown IDs from the company.

The temperature, a steady drumbeat of fear, was making him sweat, and he absently ran the back of his arm over the worry lines on his face.

In his side mirror, Latifah pushed the linen cart piled high with towels. With his black leather-gloved hand, he tugged the cap down to ensure it obscured his face from the CCTV cameras and stepped down from the truck.

Latifah pushed the cart up the ramp they'd put there to make it easy to offload the extra bundle they carried. He didn't say anything as he tipped the covered item out, ensuring that it landed on the soft cushion of laundry. Once empty, he pushed the cart out, and Latifah dragged it to the corner by the laundry room.

Zain shut the back of the truck and climbed into the front cabin. Latifah joined him.

They didn't speak as he rolled the van to the gates where the gateman opened the barrier and let them out. He drove gently into the late night traffic until he'd gone past the hotel, then accelerated but still keeping to the speed limits so he wouldn't attract attention.

When they arrived at the quiet country road where his third-in-command, Samuel, was waiting with the blacked-out SUV, he pulled over.

He climbed into the back of the truck and lifted the woman in the red dress. Cradling her to his chest, he carried her into the rear of the SUV. He didn't look at her face, choosing to view her as just a target rather than a pliant, fragrant woman. A woman to whom he had once devoted his life.

He changed his outfit from the uniform into a tuxedo suit outside the car.

Latifah emerged from the back of the truck dressed in a pair of black jeans, a black T-shirt, and black sports shoes.

Samuel cleared the van of any evidence that could link back to them, poured lighter fuel on the towels, and tossed a lit match at it. They had left enough bundles of cash with the laundry firm to compensate for the loss of their vehicle. He wouldn't hurt innocent bystanders to accomplish his goals.

Sliding into the back seat of SUV, Zain tugged the sleeping woman to his side, her head flopping on his shoulder. They would look like a couple coming back from a night of partying to prying eyes.

Samuel returned to the driver's position while Latifah sat in the front passenger space as they reversed away from the burning van, orange flames licking metal and lighting the night.

They headed to the airport where the private jet he had arrived in would be fuelled and waiting for his departure.

Clearing security proved easy with his diplomatic papers. Solomon stood ready with the aircrew as soon as the car pulled onto the tarmac beside the plane.

"We'll see you in Boma in forty-eight hours," Zain said to Latifah before he got out.

He had arrived in Lagos with a land crew of two men and a woman, Latifah, who had been posing as his wife. Now that they had the target, he would return to the plane with a crew of two men and a woman to avoid suspicion.

They had planned to leave Latifah behind. She would return to their base in Boma through alternative arrangements. Of his close team, she was his most trusted and also the most capable of working alone. Samuel and Solomon worked best together. He needed them as his backup in case anything went wrong. Latifah could take care of herself and used her feminine charm as a lethal weapon.

She would make sure the SUV was clean of any traces of their fingerprints and possible DNA before returning it to the car hire company tomorrow. Then, she would make her way back to base.

"Sure. I'll see you in forty-eight hours." She saluted with a nod.

"Make sure we're in the air within ten minutes," he said to Samuel. "I don't want to be grounded when the authorities get notified."

Solomon opened the passenger door, but Zain halted him when he reached inside.

"I'll take her," he said as he stepped out, carrying the bundle of perfumed, soft curves.

The warm sea breeze made his jacket flap as he took the steps up to the plane entrance.

"Welcome, sir. I hope you had a wonderful day," the captain greeted.

"Yes. Thank you." He strode down the aisle, placed the woman in a seat, strapped her in, and reclined the backrest to a sleeping position.

Then, he walked to another chair on the opposite side and settled in.

Samuel and Solomon joined him, removing their gloves as they sat in the chairs across the aisle.

Zain kept his heart rate low by regulating his breathing for the minutes they had to wait. He didn't want to appear agitated, although the time passed excruciatingly.

The air stewardess performed security demonstrations. The plane taxied down the runway and stopped.

A few seconds later, the announcement from the pilot came through the speakers. They would be taking off shortly.

He relaxed a little. Air traffic control had given permission for the flight to take off. They were just waiting for their turn on the runway behind the other aeroplanes. Murtala Mohammed Airport was a busy West African hub.

Soon enough, the engine gunned, and the jet began its ascent into the air. Bright orange and white lights illuminated Lagos against the inky night.

When they had levelled off, he tipped his seat back and closed his eyes.

"Good evening, sir. Can I get you a drink?"

The voice of the stewardess reached him.

He tried not to grit his teeth but forced a smile instead as he lifted his eyelids. He preferred not to be disturbed, but he had a persona to keep up for the sake of the mission.

"Whisky and a bottle of still water," he said.

Ten years ago, he wouldn't even look at the stuff let alone drink it. But he was no longer that clean-cut teetotal man. Life had stripped him of the rose-tinted view of the world.

She walked away to do his bidding.

Another announcement came over the speakers. Two hours until they would arrive in Tambao. Tambao was an airstrip that served the Tamba Manganese mines of Burkina Faso. From there, they would drive across the border into the

Republic of Wanai and to their home in Boma where the second phase of their plan would begin.

CHAPTER NINE

ISHA woke with a marching band stomping across her brain. Or she could be dead, judging by the halo of white light surrounding her. She squeezed her eyes shut.

No. There was no pain in Heaven.

Had she been partying too much last night and had a lot to drink? That was impossible. She never drank too much. She'd only had a glass of champagne, from what she could remember.

Was she coming down with an illness? The past few weeks had been hectic, so perhaps this was her body's way of seeking some rest.

She groaned, turning on her side to avoid the brightness. The bed sheets didn't feel as soft as the ones in her bed. Of course, this must be her hotel room.

"You're awake."

The soft female voice startled her, and her eyes flew open.

"Who are you?" she asked.

Dressed in a short-sleeved flared green gown, black leggings, and sandals, the woman standing on the other side of the bed couldn't be hotel staff. A quick glance around the space—eggshell walls and shuttered windows—proved it wasn't her hotel room, either.

"Your Highness, my name is Aliyah. I'm here to check you over. How is your head?"

"Achy." Isha shifted, noting that she was still dressed in the red dress she had worn to the party. She remembered being with Amara and Joya, going out to take a call. Then, nothing. Had there been an incident? "Where am I? What happened?"

"Have this." Aliyah poured water from a bottle that had been sitting on a dark bedside cabinet into a tall glass. She pulled a white packet from her pocket, showing a brand of painkiller. "This will help with your headache."

Isha swung her feet over the side of the bed. Used to having an attendant cater to her whims, Aliyah's presence didn't unsettle her as such.

But the gap in her memory made her uneasy, as well as the strange surroundings. Hopefully, the painkiller would help to resolve her temporary amnesia. She took the offerings from Aliyah, swallowing the pills and chasing them with the cold water.

"Are you a doctor? Is this a hospital?" she asked after she had returned the glass to Aliyah.

"No. This is not a hospital. I'm a junior doctor at the Teaching Hospital, which is in town."

"You mean Lagos University Teaching Hospital?"

"No. This is Wanai, not Nigeria."

"Wanai?" She frowned. "How?"

She stopped, not wanting to sound too confused in the presence of a stranger and in her fiancé's country. Etiquettes drummed into her mind since childhood meant she never wanted to give the wrong impression. The woman probably thought she had a hangover, which would be cause for gossip. Never a good thing.

"Is my fiancé here?" Her stomach churned at the thought of not looking presentable in front of Kweku.

Another downside to being a royal princess. Not just any royal princess but the prime princess of the Kingdom of Bagumi. She could never have an off day. The world always had to see the sophisticated and composed woman.

Tedious. However, she'd promised her parents she would not bring shame to her family name like she'd almost done ten years ago. The wild, reckless, spirited girl had been locked away, never to be resurrected.

She grabbed the glass of water and sipped to quench her parched throat. "You know what. Just show me to the bathroom so that I can clean up."

Returning the tumbler to the table, she glanced around the room.

With none of her luggage in sight, she assumed her items had been unpacked into the drawers and wardrobe.

"The bathroom is over there." Aliyah pointed at an adjoining door. "I can sort breakfast for you while you're cleaning up."

Isha was going to ask if she wasn't having breakfast with Kweku but closed her mouth. She didn't want to come across as clueless. "Good. I'd like scrambled eggs with egg whites only and warm croissants. If there are no croissants, then get me crust-less brown bread mildly toasted. And a pot of coffee."

She walked into the bathroom, the hard, smooth concrete floor cool under her toes.

The room was medium-sized, not as grand as the one she'd previously stayed in during her visit to the Wanai Presidential Palace.

And the lacklustre decor continued in the clean bathroom which had simple chrome taps and white units, unlike the gold-plated valves and faucets in Kweku's residence.

The excessive gold on display had seemed gaudy and distasteful. Then again, as the home of the President of Wanai, they were entitled to be surrounded by opulence and grandeur.

Here, everything functioned as they should, and she managed to brush her teeth using the new pack of toothbrush and minty paste. She wrapped her tresses into a bun at the top of her head to avoid getting them wet and stripped her clothing before she stepped into the glass enclosure. Warm water cascaded from the chrome shower head when she turned the faucet. After washing, she took a large black towel from the folded pile in the corner of the counter and dried her body.

Now that she'd showered, her headache had cleared a little, the medicine effective. She could find her purse and her phone and speak to Joya and Amara about last night. Had it been last night? It had to be because the dress lay on the bathroom floor.

Aliyah was not in the bedroom.

Isha glanced around, still not spotting her purse. It had to be in a drawer.

She opened the one closest to her, revealing assorted female underwear. Not hers.

She twisted her lips and opened another, and another.

She recognised none of the feminine clothes. Ordinary women's clothes. Nothing suitable for a princess. Nothing of hers.

What was going on? Why would Kweku accommodate her in another woman's room? Come to think of it, this shabby chamber looked like the staff quarters.

She stiffened as her mind raced, trying to piece the puzzle together.

She couldn't find her purse or her belongings. And she had slept in a stranger's bed.

She swivelled, walked to the door, and halted.

Covered only in a towel, she couldn't allow strangers to see her in a state of undress.

Then again, none of the clothes she'd seen was suitable for her. She hurried into the bathroom and picked the red dress. She wouldn't bother with the used underwear since the dress would keep her looking decent while she got answers.

A quick search didn't turn up any powder, mascara, or lipstick.

When she was in her private residence, she didn't need the extra layer. She could be herself.

She glanced at her reflection in the mirror. Frown lines marred her forehead.

She had always worn makeup in public or away from home. Applying the layers worked like a mask that kept her distant and projected the princess persona that the people adored.

Now, it felt she felt like she'd been stripped of her armour.

The clean-faced woman in the mirror looked young and inexperienced, like that girl from long ago. Her insides quivered, and her hands trembled.

Don't go there.

Turning away from reflection, she closed her eyes and sucked in a deep breath. Then, she straightened her shoulders. The world wouldn't end because she had no makeup.

She stepped out of the bathroom just as Aliyah returned with a plastic tray laden with covered dishes and cutlery.

"There you are," she said as the other woman placed the tray on the table.

Aliyah looked up at her. "Your Highness, was the shower not working?"

"The shower was working fine. I've already had a wash. But I can't find any of my clothes."

"I know the clothes here are not what you're used to, but they are nice," the woman said in a tentative voice.

"They are not my clothes. Where are my clothes?" She wouldn't wear clothes that someone else had worn.

"They didn't arrive with you."

"They didn't?"

Although she couldn't remember all of last night, one thing remained certain. She didn't do anything on impulse or haphazardly. Her life was regimented and planned to the last second. She wouldn't take an international trip even across West African nations without personal items. And while people were known to lose their baggage in transit, such a thing had never happened to her. She travelled with diplomatic clearance, and her entourage ensured a hassle-free journey.

"No."

Perhaps her luggage was stuck in transit.

She blew out air in mild irritation. "Okay. I probably have to do some shopping. Is there a local boutique? By the way, where is my purse?"

"There was no purse, either."

"No purse?" That was impossible. She wouldn't go anywhere without her handbag, just like she wouldn't travel without Kojo. "All right. Tell Kojo I require his presence. He probably has my items."

"Kojo? Who is that?" Aliyah scratched her cheek, eyebrows squished in confusion.

"My bodyguard, of course." When the woman's gaze clouded over, Isha added, "Don't tell me I didn't come here with my bodyguard. I don't go anywhere without him."

Not even to Wanai.

"I want to speak with my fiancé."

"I'm afraid that won't be possible, Your Highness."

"Why not?" She raised her voice. This had become ridiculous.

"Because he's not here." The woman's calm responses added to the absurdity of the situation.

Had she fallen down and hit her head? Perhaps she'd ended up in an unconscious concussed state which led her into a bizarre dreamscape?

"What the hell do you mean, he's not here? I came to Wanai with him, didn't I?" Isha flung her hands in the air, getting agitated.

Aliyah shook her head. "Sorry."

Her body flushed with heat. This had gone beyond ridiculous. "I've had enough of this nonsense."

Not waiting for Aliyah's response, she stomped to the door and yanked it open, only to be faced by two hulking men who looked precisely alike, standing guard at the entrance.

Neither of them bowed or made way. Their matching pairs of intriguing amber eyes lacked any genial warmth.

A chill run down her spine, and her chest tingled with dread.

Where was she? What insolence. Nobody treated her like this—they wouldn't even dare.

"Get out of my way," she ordered as she glared at them.

"We can't do that, madam," the one on the left said in a deep rumbling voice.

"Go back into the room, lady," the one on the right added. His voice was raspy.

Neither of them had addressed her formally or even correctly. The gall of them. In times past, servants would be tried for treason for less.

"I am First Princess Isha Saene of the Kingdom of Bagumi, and I demand to see my fiancé Kweku Doona immediately."

They both stiffened as if she'd punched them.

The one on the left leaned forward and lowered his voice as his eyes sparked with unfriendly fire. "Madam, there are some names you don't mention in this house, and that is one of them."

What the freaking Hell did that mean?

She straightened to her full height of five-foot-six on bare feet. Her head might only reach their chest, but she wouldn't be intimidated or disrespected by mere employees, even if they looked like they could snuff the life out of her with those giant hands of theirs.

"Did you not hear me?" She hardened her voice, injecting all the haughtiness she could muster.

"Yes, we heard you, First Princess Isha Saene of the Kingdom of Bagumi. You still have to go back into the room and stay there," the one on the right said in a surprisingly calm voice.

Aliyah appeared at her side, crossing and uncrossing her arms as she cleared her throat. "Please, Your Highness. I will explain the situation as much as I can. Please, come inside."

Isha turned her glare on Aliyah who pleaded with her eyes as well as her voice.

She couldn't force her way through the solid wall of men, even if she tried. Aliyah seemed a safer companion than those two.

"I'm not done with the two of you yet," she said in a sharp voice before swivelling and pacing across to where the open window overlooked a large courtyard enclosed by high concrete. Two men in camouflage uniforms, carrying what looked like AK47 machine guns, stopped at the far wall and stood to chat while one of them smoked a cigarette.

Seeing security officers with weapons proved to be a daily occurrence in her life, so the sight in itself didn't cause alarm.

However, taking into account her seeming amnesia, the loss of her luggage, and the not-too-friendly men guarding her room, the worm of unease settled in her stomach.

"Are you okay, My Princess?" Aliyah said in a soft voice.

Isha took calming breaths, shifting her gaze to the woman. "Yes. You have to tell me what's going on. Right now."

Aliyah brushed down her dress before folding her arms across her chest. She cleared her throat again. "Last night, you were at a party. Do you remember?"

"Yes. The pre-bachelorette event that my friends organised. I don't remember getting here. How did I get to Wanai?"

"At the party, you were taken by some people and brought here overnight."

The worm in her gut curled tight, and nausea swelled. She swallowed down bile.

"What people?"

"The Movement for the Liberation of Ganuri."

Isha's heart nearly exploded out of her chest. Swaying, she leaned on the window sill, clutched her midriff, and tried to process the woman's words.

An abduction. She'd been taken, against her will.

The Movement for the Liberation of Ganuri, or MLG for short, wanted to create a separate country from the Ganuri region of Wanai. Her fiancé Kweku was the son of the president of Wanai.

Freaking Hell! This was bad.

Bagumi was a peaceful kingdom, and the royal household was treated like a national treasure.

She had always taken her safety for granted and had never felt in danger with the team assigned to ensure her wellbeing.

It seemed her engagement to Kweku had turned her into a target for the people of Wanai.

The woman in her wanted to freak out as her heart thumped hard in her chest and her hands turned clammy.

Over the past ten years, she had trained her mind and learned to suppress the woman and lock her emotions out of sight.

She presented the stoic princess to the world to save her heart from being shattered again. She needed the play to that defiance at this moment.

"Why? What do they want from me? Are you one of them?" The questions came out almost jumbled up as her mind raced.

She could imagine that they might want to use her as a bargaining chip due to her engagement to the son of the president of the country they wanted to split.

"Yes, I am a member of the MLG, and we want what we've always wanted, to be free. And you're going to help us gain our freedom."

Isha's mouth fell open, taken aback by the calm certainty in Aliyah's voice. The woman showed no fear, and her eyes were bright with a zealousness that she hadn't witnessed in years.

Her ribs squeezed tight. She envied the woman's total belief in her cause. She hadn't felt real passion for anything in a decade.

No. Her dedication to the Royal House of Saene, to the people of Bagumi and soon to the people of Wanai, was enough passion.

And that dedication meant she couldn't show any fear or sympathy to Aliyah or the MLG.

She straightened her shoulders and tilted her chin up. "The Royal House of Saene does not negotiate with terrorists. I am sure the same applies to the Federal Government of Wanai. Holding me hostage will only ensure that you are all arrested and executed. But I am willing to overlook the abduction if you let me go. As a matter of fact, I demand that you release me right away."

"You are in no position to demand anything."

That voice—thick, smooth, and masculine. There was no mistaking the speaker, although she hadn't heard him in years.

It couldn't be.

Isha whirled around. A wave of dizziness passed over her as she stared at the man occupying the entrance to the room. She hadn't heard the door open. Perhaps Aliyah hadn't shut it.

"Zain."

She stumbled backwards as his name came out in a hoarse whisper through her clogged throat. The back of her legs hit the bed frame, and she slumped on the mattress.

There was no doubt of who she stared at.

The man she remembered had matured—thick afro shaved to the scalp at the sides and back, trimmed hairs running down the sides, upper lip, and chin of his walnut-hued face, framing lush, plump lips.

Those lips stayed in a tight line just as his dark, piercing eyes—usually hot ebony, now seeming as cold as granite—sending more chills down her back.

The clean-cut suits he'd sported when she'd known him—had she ever really known him?—had been replaced by these dark green cargo trousers and grey linen shirt worn by a man who seemed more at home in the jungle than in a classroom.

At least, he didn't wield any visible weapons. Although, any threats against her would prove to be more psychological than physical from past experience.

"I'm sorry," Aliyah said before she walked over to Zain. "Is it okay to head to the hospital now?"

"Of course. Thank you for your help." Zain pressed a kiss to her forehead before she walked out of the door.

Isha's gut twisted at the intimate exchange between the two, and she turned away.

The quiet click of the shutting door galvanised her, and she shot to her feet. The room closed around her, making her claustrophobic as her heart raced, and her skin grew clammy.

She couldn't stay in the same room with *that* man.

No. No. No.

Finding her shoes beside wardrobe, she straightened them and slipped her feet in. Then, she clipped the buckles of the straps.

The height of the stiletto meant she at least seemed to be eye to eye with Zain, although she avoided his gaze following her every movement.

"Do you have my purse?"

He shrugged. "You didn't have it on your person last night."

Of course, she remembered now. She'd gone to the ladies' after taking the call from Kweku, and the woman had injected her with something that had sent her to sleep.

She gritted her teeth and puffed out a breath.

"Then you have to arrange for me to be returned to Bagumi immediately." She paused and rethought. "Just give me a phone, and I'll call the palace to send Papa's plane to pick me up. I'm sure they'll send one right away."

She focused on the practical. It saved from thinking about the man and his reasons for taking her.

Kojo would probably come with the plane. Oh, Kojo. What had happened to her trusted bodyguard?

"I hope you didn't hurt Kojo." She still didn't meet his gaze.

If she didn't look at him, then she didn't have to acknowledge his presence. Didn't have to recognise a whole lot of other things she didn't want to delve into.

"If you mean your bodyguard, then no, we didn't hurt him."

"Good." She nodded. "Then bring me a phone. The sooner I make the call, the sooner I can get out of here and forget that this ever happened."

Most of all, she wanted to scrub him from her mind. To lose the awareness of him in the same room, standing only a few feet away. Just a couple of steps and she could touch him.

No! Don't go there. If you touch him, it should be a slap for what he did to you, for what he is doing to you.

She wouldn't.

Slapping him would be more devastating for her than him. It would be an acknowledgement of their history. A history she had tried hard to scrub out of her mind and life.

He didn't say anything for seconds that ticked into minutes.

From the corner of her eye, she spied him.

He stood there, still, composed, immovable, implacable.

He wanted something from her. She could tell. A concession.

Funny, because there'd been a time she had given this man everything, and it hadn't been enough.

Her heart raced. She clenched her hands and unclenched them.

She needed to get away from him. She didn't trust herself with him.

Surely, he understood the consequences of detaining her spelt death for him.

Finally, she straightened her shoulders and lifted her head, keeping her chin up in an imperious pose.

Something flashed in his gaze before it hardened again. Satisfaction? Was he happy that she'd met his gaze?

"Mr. Bassong, if you will, please arrange for a phone to be sent to me. I will like to rest now. You are dismissed."

He burst out laughing, a cold, echoing mirth that didn't reach his eyes and chilled her to the bones.

As quickly as it started, the laughter died, and he took a step in her direction.

Her impulse was to step back, but she hadn't done anything impulsive in years. A princess, especially the First Princess, could never give in to impulse. She stayed where she stood as he advanced.

"First Princess Isha Ruby—"

"Don't call me that!" She couldn't stop the vulnerable thrumming or the vehemence in her voice when he used her middle name. Her gut wrenched, and the throbbing returned to her temples.

He jerked back and raised one dark brow.

"Is that not your name, Ruby Bagumi?"

The tone of his voice baited her, and his rigid posture mocked her.

She stiffened her spine and squared her shoulders. "You know very well that I am the First Princess of the Kingdom of Bagumi, and my given name is Isha Saene. You can address me as Your Highness or Princess Isha."

"Oh." He tilted his head and scratched the hair on his chin. "Ten years ago, I met a student in London. She was beautiful, intelligent, compassionate, or at least, I'd thought she was at the time. She had these brilliant ideas that could change the world. She told me her name was Ruby Bagumi. But I found out it was a lie."

He cut her open with his words, a thousand paper-cuts, making her bleed from her soul.

She closed her eyes tight and balled her fists.

She would not go there, would not bleed for him to see.

I am First Princess Isha Saene, she recited in her mind. Isha Saene.

"I am First Princess Isha Saene," she said out loud and took a deep breath as she opened her eyes.

He stood close. If she reached out, she could place her palm on his chest. Was his heart thumping as hard as hers? His scent clung in the air, cedar wood and citrus, tantalising her with each breath.

Memories she'd locked away hovered, threatening to break free.

Nails biting into her palms, she took a step back. "I demand a phone call."

"So that's the way you want to play it." He nodded, moving away as he made his proclamation. "First Princess Isha Saene of the Kingdom of Bagumi, you are now a captive of the MLG group. You will remain in our custody until our grievances are met. As for your *demand*—" he spat out the word as if it were offensive "—you have no power and no rights here. This is Wanai where the supreme power remains with the supreme leader, and in this region, *I* am the supreme leader. You will do as you are told while you are here."

"I will not," she retorted, bristling that he dared to make such a declaration. "I do not submit to your leadership. The only authorities I recognise are my father, His Majesty the King of Bagumi, and Almighty God."

He gave the bitter laughter again, the one that sent shivers down her spine.

"You are engaged to a Wanaian man. What do you think will happen after you are wedded? In Wanai, your husband will have total authority over you."

Her chin jutted as she glared at him. "Kweku and anyone else will be out of their freaking minds if they think I'm going to abide by that antiquated edict."

Her mother would blanch in horror if she heard Isha speak in this manner. Language suited only to commoners. Still, this man made her forget herself and her upbringing every time.

"*There she is*. There is the woman I once knew as Ruby Bagumi." For the first time, a small smile tugged the corner of his lips. "Welcome to Wanai. Make yourself comfortable. Well, as comfortable as you can under the circumstances. I'll see you again soon."

He whirled around and was gone before she could respond.

Her chest heaved as she tried to catch her breath and make sense of what had just happened.

Why was Zain doing this to her now?

And worse—why was he set on resurrecting the past?

CHAPTER TEN

ZAIN'S smile wavered as he strode down the hallway. Light filled the space, coming through the bay windows at the end.

His plans had been activated.

Isha was here, in his house.

He should be happy.

But being near her had reawakened old feelings. Feelings he'd thought he'd buried years ago.

It didn't help that she proved reluctant to acknowledge their shared past.

He pushed open the door to his study and walked in, letting it swing shut before he leaned against it.

Sucking in a deep breath, he closed his eyes.

It didn't help that he remembered the beat of her heart and the warmth of her skin. He yearned to have her back in his arms. First, he would spank her for all the troubles she had caused. Then, he would kiss her until she became out of breath.

Afterwards, he would lick and taste every inch and crevice of her delicious, naked body, from her delicate neck to her full breasts, from her sensitive earlobes to the broad sweep of her hips, from the dip of her belly button to her smooth, slender legs.

He let out a long groan as his body reacted to the fantasy.

Why couldn't he stop thinking about her?

Ten years, and Isha still held sway over his thoughts and his body. She made him feel young and reckless.

He let out a bark of laughter as he opened his eyes and walked to the balcony. At almost forty years old, he'd left his youth behind and could not afford to be reckless. He should be preparing for a meeting. Instead, he thought about a woman when the lives of so many depended on him.

He sucked in another deep breath and centred himself. This view always grounded him.

From his hillside perch, he overlooked the town of Boma, green foliage of trees and red zinc roofs on cream-coloured concrete buildings stretched over the valley.

The edifice of his modest home was surrounded by high walls and trees—almonds, mangos, and cashew.

In the distance, beyond the sedate city, was the blue shimmer of the Atlantic Ocean.

The air lay motionless, creating the feel of a solid mass hanging over the shimmery landscape. The sun bore down, radiating oppressive heat in the stillness. At midmorning, the temperature of the day was yet to hit its peak. In the distance, dark clouds loomed. They had hours, perhaps, until they'd have a downpour.

His loose linen clothing helped to keep him fresh as he returned into his quarters. Slatted blinds shielded the space from most of the sun and kept the interior temperate. A soft aura of light came in from the shaded windows, giving the brown leather chairs and dark wood furniture an earthy haze.

Although air conditioners were installed in the building, he refused to have them turned on, not when there were people in the town who couldn't afford to have their homes cooled in the same way.

For weeks, the region had been under siege from economic sanctions imposed by the federal government. The current fuel scarcity had resulted in over one hundred per cent inflation.

All of this had been designed to punish the Ganuri people for daring to want their own nation and sovereignty.

Boma had been a thriving city well before the arrival of the Europeans. It had been a trade centre connecting the coastal West African nations as well as the northern tribes.

Afterwards, it had become a seaport and a significant point in the transatlantic trade and had since turned into a major harbour in Wanai. But even that had been taken away as the federal government had banned shipping companies from stopping at Boma and closed down the terminal.

They wanted Zain to give up on his cause, but this was his ancestral home. The Ganuri were his people. Their blood ran in his veins, and he had no other primary purpose than to fight for his people.

A tapping sound drew his attention.

"Come," he said as he turned around.

The panel slid open, and Samuel stood just beyond the threshold. He entered, followed by Solomon. Solomon toured the room, doing a survey with his handheld wiretap detector. When he completed a full circle, he nodded at Zain, and they all sat down around the table.

A bug sweep had to be done before any crucial meetings. It wasn't that he didn't trust the people around him. But he would be naive to think that there weren't spies around, just like he had spies in the other camp.

He picked up the remote control from the table and pressed the power button to turn on the screen on the wall to the side of his desk, which had a camera clipped to the top so it could view the occupants of the room. The small arrow on the monitor turned in a continuous circle for a few seconds before the connection was made on the voice-over-IP software.

A dark-skinned man in a navy blue shirt appeared on the screen in a sitting position, outlined against a plain grey wall behind. Shafts of light from the sun cut across the background.

"Good morning, Uncle," Zain said in greeting.

"Good morning, sir," Samuel and Solomon added.

"Good morning, Zain, Samuel, Solomon." Uncle Jeremiah was his mother's brother and a Lieutenant General in Wanai's army. The man's gaze went across the room from one man to the next. "Where is Latifah?"

He was also Latifah's father.

"She hasn't arrived yet. We're expecting her to check in any moment now."

As if on cue, the satellite phone on the table trilled, and Samuel pressed the button to put it on speaker.

"Hello," Solomon spoke.

"It's me." Latifah's voice was easy recognisable over the crackly metallic connection. "Can't chat for long. I got delayed but will be crossing soon. There are no birds on the wire, but there are more dogs and fences. Also, I've got a guide so I should be fine. We'll see you soon."

The line went dead. She had purposefully ended the call quickly so that if by any chance she had picked up a trace, it wouldn't detect their location. And her words had been mostly in code and sounded innocent enough to any listener.

"Did you get that, Uncle?" Zain asked.

"Not very well. The line was bad on this end."

"She said she got delayed, but she will be crossing the border soon. There's no news in the media, but there are more patrols and checkpoints."

"Did she say she's got a guide?"

"Yes. That means she's got someone with her."

"Who?"

"I don't know. Could be someone helping her. Then again, she said 'we'll see you soon'."

"Which means she's bringing the person here," Samuel interjected. "That wasn't part of the plan."

"It wasn't, but we trust her, don't we? She is very resourceful and will never put our objectives in jeopardy. So I'm going to wait until I see her and find out what's going on," Zain said.

Latifah was the one he trusted the most. She had worked in the country's military intelligence. She would kill herself instead of bringing an enemy into their camp on purpose.

"I agree," Uncle Jeremiah said. "Latifah is capable of getting herself out of dicey situations. I trust her actions are for the best."

"Of course," Samuel said.

The older man cleared his throat. "I do have news for you. Not good. I was in a meeting yesterday, and there was talk of sending troops into Ganuri Delta and ultimately Boma."

Zain stiffened and shook his head. He had known what could be on the cards since the embargo had started. They already had more checkpoints on major roads into the region.

"That will be an invasion and a declaration of war," Solomon said sharply, echoing Zain's thoughts.

"They are going to couch it as preventing violence."

"Preventing violence? Where was the army when AK47-totting cattle-rearers were invading villages and killing locals? Thousands of people displaced from their homes in what amounts to ethnic cleansing, and they did nothing. Now that we've mounted our own militants to protect the citizens, they want to invade us?" Samuel's rage was evident as his eyes blazed.

"They say your actions are not legal. You are not the armed forces or the police. You cannot keep the peace."

"But we have kept the peace."

"Sam, I know you're angry. But you have to calm down. Let's get all the facts and decide what to do."

Samuel swallowed and nodded.

Zain turned back to the screen. "Has the order been issued?"

"Not to my knowledge. There will be a meeting of the Chiefs of Staff with the Head of State next week to make the order official."

"Okay." He nodded as his mind whirled. He had prepared for this day. Yet, now that it stared him in the face, he proved reluctant to take the actions, knowing the consequence would be severe for his people.

"When we embarked on this journey, we knew a day like this might arise, and we planned for this day. Now, we must put those plans into action. I know we have all been on the same page on the previous action. But it is one thing to spout an ideology and quite another to pick up arms to defend said ideology. So I want to give everyone in this room and of course you, as well, Uncle, the chance to excuse themselves."

The older man covered his mouth with his hand as he coughed.

"You know I have always supported your ideas, son. And I will continue to do so in whatever form I can. But as a serving member of the Wanai armed forces, I will be on the opposing side if you go ahead with your actions. I cannot be seen to help you."

"I totally understand, Uncle. You have been of immense help so far, and I am always grateful."

"Your father was a great man. He will be very proud of you, just as I am."

"Thank you, Uncle."

Zain was almost glad the man wasn't doing much more than passing vital information. As it was, his actions could be classified as treason and could result in his execution. He already had so much family tragedy. He didn't want any more.

"I have to go. May the Almighty guide your actions and guard your way. Viva Ganuri. Viva Wanai."

"Viva Ganuri. Viva Wanai," the men around the table chanted before the screen turned to a pale blue.

Zain closed his eyes and exhaled a breath. With his next few words, he would be making a significant change in his life. Although technically, the move had manifested over time.

As a lawyer, he'd become a man of ideas and law and subsequently a defender of his people, first in the courts and then in the media, using the rules of his land as the tools to accomplish his task. But that hadn't been enough. He had organised protests, led rallies, and had gotten arrested on several occasions. Intervention from international human rights campaigners had ensured his release on quite a few of those times. Now, he had transformed into something else, a man of action, and a general, ready to call other men to raise arms and defend their land.

He'd had to call men to arms over twelve months ago when the villages started getting invaded by gunmen who raped and pillaged. The government hadn't done anything. When they'd sent the military, it had been after lives and properties had been lost. People had run away from their homes and had ended up in refugee camps.

Refugees in their own country, damn it!

Because their government didn't care about their plights more than delivering sound bites.

So he'd recruited and trained men, sourced weapons and armed them and sent them on patrols around the towns and village. The killings from gunmen invasions had been reduced since, and they hadn't had any new attacks in weeks. Hopefully, it would stay that way.

Opening his eyes, he shifted in his seat to face the two men sitting across the table from him.

Actually, he wasn't a general. Samuel and Solomon were his generals. Their speciality had been forged in the fires of the Sierra Leonean war and afterwards refined with training from some of the world's best retired military experts.

While Latifah had the precision of a surgeon's scalpel, the twins were the butcher's double-edged cleaver.

He'd hoped he wouldn't need their brute forces, but it looked like their time approached.

"How many men do we have available?" he asked.

"We have about two thousand fully trained, and another thirty-five hundred who are in the process of training," Samuel replied. He led the team turning the recruits into soldiers.

Zain nodded. He would love to wait until everyone was ready, but they might be out of time. "What about the weapons. Do we have enough to arm all the men?"

"Not nearly enough," Solomon said. "But we have a shipment due in tomorrow."

"Make sure that shipment gets here. Doona is going to try to cut us off and keep us isolated. Also, make sure our naval defences are fully functional. We don't want to be taken by surprise."

"Already in place," Solomon said. "The men are ready to be deployed along the city battlements and to secure the checkpoints around Boma."

"And I will make sure we have the rest of the region covered," Samuel added.

"Good. But before we go to all-out war, I still have one last card to play."

"Do you think it will work?"

"All we have is hope."

Because the alternative was war and death. And he would like to avoid that outcome if he could help it.

CHAPTER ELEVEN

BY noon, grey clouds battled with blue skies over Boma.

On her previous trips to Wanai, Isha hadn't been here. It lacked the frenetic energy she'd witnessed in the other major Wanaian cities.

She stood by the window overlooking the balcony and the city below. She had already tried the door handles—the one out into the corridor and the one into the gallery—so she could go outside. They were locked.

The glass louvres in wooden frames made the thought of going out through the windows near impossible. She hadn't yet figured out how to take out the individual slats.

What would be the point?

Armed men patrolled the perimeter of the compound. If she managed to get out onto the balcony and climb down safely, she would still have to get past security.

No. Her best chance was to wait for Aliyah to come back. She doubted she could convince Zain, and she didn't look forward to seeing him again.

Aliyah had appeared sympathetic earlier. Perhaps she could play to that kindness.

Why had she thought this was the presidential palace earlier? This house had none of the gleaming towers or grandeur. Its position on a hill protected by cliffs and the ruins of the old Nubian city walls gave it the feel of an impenetrable fort.

The tranquil view projected a kaleidoscope of colour—an exquisite oil painting. With the red earth as a foundation, the turquoise sea shimmered against azure skies to the south while emerald rain forest occupied the west, and at its heart, the cream and red homes of the locals.

"You are exquisite, a jewel amongst stones, just like Boma. I will take you there someday so you can see exactly what I mean."

The promise flashed in her mind as if it had just been uttered.

Her heart rate picked up, and her knees went weak as the shock of seeing Zain after so many years returned. She'd heard his voice. Been in the same room with him.

Whoosh. Whoosh. Whoosh.

The sound of her racing heart filled her ears.

This had to be his house. This was his city, his hometown.

Zain had spoken the truth about Boma. It was beautiful. He had also kept his promise of bringing her here, although she hadn't imagined she would be forced here as his prisoner.

Why had he taken her after so many years?

"Do not contact me again."

Her heart wrenched as she remembered those words on the screen of her laptop.

She gripped the wooden window sill and clenched her teeth. No, she wouldn't cry.

Hate. That was the emotion she should summon. The sentiment she had carried for years against one person.

Against Zain.

He didn't deserve anything else.

A hard knock on wood startled her out of her thoughts. Hand to her chest, she swivelled just as the door swung open.

Zain stood in the space under the wooden frame.

Sucking in a sharp breath, she stood in the middle of the bedroom and stared at him, unprepared to see him again so soon after the last time, which had to be only a few hours.

He stared at her, too, as if unable to do anything else, his body taut and towering as it occupied most of the doorway.

Even without his trademark suits, his devastating appearance still caused a tremor in her body.

His hands clenched into fists at his side.

The motion got her brain into active mode.

"What do you want?" she asked in a hard tone.

"You," he said, his tone edged with huskiness.

Her heart skipped a beat.

"W—what?" she stuttered as nervousness pulsed through her.

The last time she'd heard him utter a similar phrase, he'd been a young professor, the youngest she'd encountered as a law student. He'd been bookish, tall, slender, fine, so damn fine. He'd also been an activist with a susceptible heart and exuberant smile, keen to educate young minds and impart innovative ideas.

In the intervening years, he'd taken his campaign from the classroom to the courtroom.

He had changed. Gone was the youthful exuberance and mirth, replaced by the danger and darkness of ruthless eyes, tightly-controlled rugged face, and finely-honed muscles and the strength of a warrior.

Something fluttered low in her belly. A yearning sparked to life.

No. She gritted her teeth. Where was her hatred for him? That was the only emotion he deserved from her.

She turned her head away. All that mattered was for her to get out of here. In a few weeks, she would be married to Kweku, and this blip in her life would be forgotten.

"I came to invite you to lunch."

His deep voice snagged her attention.

She couldn't help the hysterical laughter bubbling out of her.

"Invite me to lunch. Is that what this is? Was I *invited* to your house?" Animated by anger, she paced, glancing at him occasionally. "Did you send an email? No? An SMS? A message with my assistant? Perhaps she forgot to tell me. Or wait. It must have been a telegram, right? You see, that is so nineteenth century. We are in the twenty-first—"

She paced to the far wall, turned, and halted.

Zain strode across the room.

On reflex, she stepped away.

He kept coming towards her.

Her back hit the concrete of the wall.

He stood before her, looming dangerously, dark eyes gleaming.

So close. Too close.

She sucked in a deep breath. Her nostrils filled with his alluring cologne—citrus and cedar wood—the same one that she'd always loved and made her want to take in a lungful of him.

"What are you doing?" she challenged.

"I'm going to kiss you. Or perhaps I should spank you." He leaned forward.

Her pulse rate skyrocketed, and her mouth watered. She pressed her hands to the wall, hoping to hide their trembling.

"You wouldn't dare," she shot out. "I'm engaged to another man."

"Wouldn't I?" One dark eyebrow arched, and he looked her over.

He took another step, demolishing any space left between them, his palms braced on the façade, on both sides of her face.

His hardness and heat pressed against her flesh, the clothes seeming no barrier as his mouth descended.

She swallowed, scrambling in her brain for a way to repel him. If he followed through with his promise, she would be lost.

"Zain, let me go, right this minute, or I swear you will hang for this," she said in a hoarse voice as her throat clogged up.

He halted, his mouth only a whisker away and tilted his head so he could meet her gaze.

"I'm ready to die for the people I love. Can you say the same, Princess?"

He claimed her then, his lips on hers, firm and insistent.

She resisted, for all of ... she didn't know how long. Just that she lifted her hands to push him away.

The tip of his tongue brushed along her rim. One hand gripping her nape, the other pads of his fingers brushed behind her left earlobe, sending a bolt of desire to her core.

Her fingers curled around the fabric of his shirt, and she moaned and opened to him.

Without hesitation, he delved in, sweeping and searing. Plundering.

Pleasure awoke, untamed and overwhelming, just like it had always been between them. No. Different. This time was hot and dark, more than she remembered.

Somewhere in her mind, a red light was blinking. A warning. This was wrong.

The wild part of her that she had buried took over, extinguishing the alert, and she allowed herself to feel, sinking into the waves of desire.

This was Zain. Her Professor Bassong.

Once upon a time, she had claimed him, just as he had claimed her.

She had wanted to put her stamp all over him. For him to wear her mark. For the world to know that he belonged to her.

The desperate need came alive again, and she let it consume her. No man had ever kissed her like this, touched her like this, and possessed her like this.

She entwined her tongue with his and pressed her chest against his. Her nipples tightened like bullet tips, her breasts aching. Her nerve endings sizzled.

His groan rumbled through her.

And then, his kiss gentled.

His slow caress slew her, weakened her.

The flash of alarm returned.

What was she doing? She couldn't be weak. Not for Zain. Not again.

She stiffened.

He must have noticed the change in her because he lifted his head. "Princess?"

"I can't."

Her voice sounded breathless. She looked away, afraid of being weakened again.

"You can't have lunch with me?" he asked.

She shook her head. She had almost forgotten his request, which seemed like it had been made months rather than minutes ago.

He stepped back. "Shame. Mama will be disappointed."

She jerked. "Your mum? She's here?"

"Of course she's here. It's her house, too."

"Oh. Of course." She licked her dry lips. "Sure. I'd like to join you for lunch."

Did his mother know that he kept her as a hostage? Did she support his actions? Surely, no mother could condone those deeds.

"Good. You might want to change your dress, though. Lunch is a simple affair, and we're not big on ceremony around here, as you can see." He waved at his very casual attire. "There are new clothes in the wardrobe."

"Clothes that belong to your girlfriend."

Or was Aliyah his wife? In this part of the world, a man of his age would be married. And so would a woman of Aliyah's age, especially if they were living under the same roof. The separate rooms didn't fool her. Couples in certain social classes were known to sleep in different chambers.

He ignored her outburst and strode to the wardrobe, opening it.

"The clothes are clean and suitable for the occasion." He pulled one out of the selection still in a cellophane wrapper. "This one looks lovely. Would you like me to help you get changed?"

Her cheeks heated. "Of course not. I do not require your help."

"As you wish." He tilted his head slightly and glanced at his watch. "Lunch will be ready in thirty minutes. I'll be back to get you."

He pulled the door ajar and walked away.

In the ensuing silence, her thoughts resurfaced.

He hadn't denied her accusation about Aliyah being his girlfriend.

A bolt of annoyance went through her. How dare he? He had kissed her while he had another woman.

Was she any better? She had returned his kiss while engaged to another man.

She picked up the dress, ready to sling it against the wall. White tags dangled from the hem.

She tore off the cellophane. It was a new dress, unused and expensive, too, considering the quality of the navy linen and intricate leaf embroidery all over. It must have taken ages to sew the amount of delicate detailing.

Without thinking, she undressed, letting the red silk and chiffon ball gown drop to the floor, and tugged the shift dress over her head. She pulled the zipper up and walked to the mirror she had seen inside the door of the open wardrobe.

The beautiful dress was an exact fit, skimming her curves and complimenting her dark skin tone. It was as if it had been chosen for her.

Something niggled at her, and she opened the drawers again, noticing the unopened packs of toiletries and feminine products. On closer inspection, the lingerie proved to still have shop tags, too. They had never been used.

Every item of clothing or personal products was new.

Had Zain bought them for her?

No. More likely that Aliyah had done the shopping.

Her abduction hadn't been a random event. Zain had planned and prepared for her arrival long before she had.

Chapter Twelve

THIRTY minutes later, two short taps on the door alerted her to a presence.

Isha sashayed to it, the heels of the leather sandals she'd found in the wardrobe slapping against the tiles. She'd managed to find pins to hold her hair away from her face neatly.

When she pulled it open, Zain stood in the hallway, looking like he'd arrived to take her on a date. He'd changed from the cargo trousers into a beige linen suit and white shirt.

Hot damn. He was a devastatingly handsome man.

Her breath caught in her throat, and she scrambled for what to say.

"You look ... smart." She swapped out the implicating 'striking' for the safer 'smart.'

"Smart?"

The smile he gave her threatened to melt her bones. Holy ruler, he still had the sexiest grin in the known world.

She licked her lip. "Well, yes. Compared to what you were wearing earlier."

"Thank you. You look beautiful." He stepped closer. "You always do whether you're wearing one of those princess-ey gowns or nothing."

Her cheeks heated as his dark gaze swept over her. She cleared her throat. "Thank you. Are you going somewhere, or did you dress up for me?"

"I've got a meeting with some governors after lunch. For you, I'd wear nothing." He winked at her.

Her cheeks heated again as the image of him without clothes entered her mind.

She needed to get a grip, or she would be in trouble.

"Come on, Mama is waiting." He waved his hand down the hall and stepped so that there was room for her to walk beside him.

A staircase split the landing into two wings, the interior space airy and quiet. It was larger than she had expected. On the walls were hand-woven rugs with intricate Nubian designs, and on plinths were sculptures that looked similar to Asante and Benin art.

Downstairs, the same designs and artefacts continued. They looked like antiquities, perhaps from the seventeenth and eighteenth centuries, although she didn't have the expertise to date them accurately.

The dining room was bright and fresh, with a full window and a whirring ceiling fan. A solid, dark wood table sat in the middle, with six matching chairs covered in upholstery.

Someone sat in the armchair nearest and backing the entrance.

Zain strode over, bent to kiss her on both cheeks as they conversed in the local Ganui language which Isha understood some.

"Good to see you here, Mama," he said as he beamed a smile on his mother.

"I'm excited because we have a guest. Where is she?" Mrs. Bassong turned in the chair, her movement stiff as if she didn't have a one-eighty-degree rotation of her neck.

Zain moved aside, so she came into full view.

Isha swallowed her shock. Mrs. Bassong had changed drastically since the last time she had seen her.

The most apparent changes were her weight loss and the mostly white, low-cut natural hair. Her hair had been all black when Isha had last seen her, and she'd had the beautiful body of a plus-size model, which had bolstered Isha's confidence considering she had always been the plump one of all her sisters.

Now, the woman was still beautiful in her blue and white patterned round-neck booboo, even though she seemed to have gone down two dress sizes. Her radiant smile was still there. She always seemed to have it.

"Are you going to stand there and stare at me?" Mrs. Bassong said in Ganui and lifted her right arm. "Or are you going to give this old lady a hug?"

Isha stepped forward and leaned down to embrace the woman. "You are not an old lady, Mrs. Bassong."

"Mrs. Bassong?" The woman glanced at her son before returning her curious gaze to Isha. "Why the formality? I thought we were past that by now. Or should I address you as Your Highness?"

Isha cheeks flamed. The woman had always been direct, and it seemed she hadn't lost that in their time apart.

"No. Of course not, Mama," she replied.

"That's better, my daughter. Now, sit. Right here." She pointed at the chair immediately to her right.

Zain walked over and pulled it out for her. He made sure she'd sat before he took his on the opposite side.

A sense of déjà vu settled on Isha, and memory tugged at her.

Once upon a time, she had enjoyed sitting in the company of these two as they ate their meals.

She shook her head. Those memories were tainted by what had come afterwards, and she didn't want to dwell on them.

A servant arrived with a tray and unloaded the dishes of Bassi-salté and Chere—seasoned meat cooked with tomato paste and vegetables and served on local millet couscous.

The aroma of the food had her stomach growling, and her mouth watered.

"You must be hungry, my dear," Mrs. Bassong commented with a smile.

"I am. I didn't eat breakfast."

Zain's mother tutted and passed her the serving spoon to help herself. "Not good. We can't have you starving."

Mrs. Bassong still hadn't moved her left arm. She glanced at Zain, who had a blank expression. Was something wrong?

Instinctively, she took the woman's plate and dished out her portion before doing the same with Zain's plate. Neither of them commented. It had seemed natural to do so because she'd done it before and also because something seemed wrong with the older woman's arm.

She served herself last and only took a small scoop of couscous, not wanting to overload on the carbohydrate.

"Surely, you're going to eat more than that," Mama said. "There's plenty, so you can help yourself to extra servings."

"This will be enough for me, Mama."

"Really? I remembered you used to compete with Zain for the extras from my Bassi-salté."

"That's because you make the best Bassi-salté ever."

Isha had never eaten the dish until Zain's mum had cooked it for her ten years ago. In those days, she hadn't been so obsessed with keeping slim. Zain had loved her curves. Not to mention that their extracurricular activities had always made her ravenous afterwards.

"She sure does," Zain said.

"Thank you." Mama beamed a smile. "So eat up."

Isha didn't need to be told. Once she started eating, she only paused to chat when Mama asked about what she'd been doing in the past few years. She spoke about her work and family but failed to mention Kweku or her engagement to him. That would not go down well with Zain or his mother. And she wanted to keep things simple and pleasant for the older woman's sake.

The woman had been kind to her, a surrogate mother of sorts when she'd spent some weeks in London while Isha had been a student there.

"I have to head off to my meeting, Mama." Zain placed his cutlery on his empty white ceramic plate. He stood and kissed his mother on the cheek. He looked at Isha but didn't come over to her. "I'll see both of you this evening."

"I hope you have a fruitful day," Mama said.

Isha didn't say anything to him as he walked out of the door. She placed her cutlery on the plate. She'd had a second helping, after all.

She used the opportunity to ask the question that had been niggling at her. "Mama, I noticed you haven't used your left arm. Are you injured?"

Mrs. Bassong let out a sigh as she leaned back. "I had a stroke months ago, and I suffered minor paralysis on my left side."

"Oh. I'm so sorry."

"Thank you. I can move my legs, but my left arm hasn't been itself since. Honestly, my body hasn't really been itself since the fall. It's been one thing or the other. The stroke was just the latest."

"That must be hard for you. I heard about the accident when—"

"Accident?" Mama's voice was sharp and bitter. "Is that what they told you? I suppose Wanai Television Authority broadcasted the news at the time."

"I'm sorry." Isha was surprised at the harshness in the woman's tone. She'd never heard her upset before. "Ten years ago, it was in the WTA news that you fell off the balcony of your home. Was that not what happened?"

The woman shook her head slowly. "I lived in this house from the day I married my husband and raised a family here. No one ever fell until the day the Wanai Secret Police showed up. He pushed me off the balcony. It was a miracle that I didn't die. My fall was broken by my husband's old car parked underneath."

"Oh, my goodness!" Isha's mouth dropped open, and then fury blazed through her. "Who did that? I hope they got punished."

"Punished?" Mama huffed. "More like he got a promotion. And if they reported it as an accident, then no one is responsible."

Her stomach curdled, and bile rose in her throat. "I'm so sorry. I didn't know. I would have ..."

She would have mentioned her intention to visit had she known. However, it would have been almost impossible at the time. She'd had her own Hell to get through in the same period.

Mrs. Bassong sighed again. "I can't blame you for not coming to see me. You didn't know, and it was not a safe time to be anywhere near this family. Doona and his secret police were bent on destroying my family. Zain had been planning to bring you to Boma before it happened. It is a good thing he didn't. I would have been upset if anything had happened to you."

Pain bloomed in Isha's chest.

She remembered the plans she and Zain had made. He'd promised to bring her here to see his beautiful Boma. It had never happened. Had it been because of the tragedy of his mother's fall?

"Do not contact me again."

No. Zain hadn't wanted anything to do with her. That was the sole reason he had kept her away.

"I'm sorry, Mama," she said, at a loss for what else to say.

"No. Don't be. None of it was your fault. I'm sad that you have to visit us under these circumstances."

She jerked back. How much did the woman know? "Mama, this isn't exactly a visit, considering how I got here."

Mama reached out her good hand and covered Isha's. "I beg you to pardon my son's actions. You see, sometimes, love is like madness. The Doonas are responsible for so many atrocities in Ganuri. And when news came that you were engaged to marry Kweku Doona, Zain was devastated."

"What?" Isha opened and closed her mouth.

"What do you expect from a man who finds out that the woman he loves is engaged to the man who threw his mother off the balcony?"

Isha bumped the table, and the cutlery clattered noisily on the crockery, her mouth agape.

She couldn't have heard the woman correctly.

Sure, she'd heard the part about Zain loving her. But she could dismiss it as false. Zain didn't cherish her.

However, the other part?

Mrs. Bassong had implied that the man who had pushed her off the balcony was Kweku Doona. Her Kweku. Impossible.

Kweku was strict but not heartless. A person needed to be tough to lead a country like Wanai. And Kweku was going to be the next president after his father because Wanai was a one-party nation and he'd get voted in. The system wasn't perfect. But it worked for them.

"Mama, I think you might be confused about who pushed you. Maybe you saw Kweku's picture on the TV, and he looked like the man on the balcony."

This had to be the explanation. The alternative ...

She shook her head.

Mrs. Bassong pursed her lips in a wry smile. "My daughter, I am not confused. Kweku Doona came to this house. He pushed me. I saw him as clearly as I'm seeing you right now."

"Oh. Lord." Isha's stomach heaved. She scrubbed her hands over her face. "Mama, I'm sorry."

She pushed the chair back and fled the dining room.

There had to be another explanation for what had happened to Mama. It couldn't be Kweku.

No, there had to be something else at play here. She just had to wait for Zain's return and demand an explanation.

Years ago when they'd met each other, although he'd been the professor and she'd been the student, he'd always allowed her to express her opinions, and he, in return, had never hidden his views from her.

Why would this have changed now?

CHAPTER THIRTEEN

ZAIN sat in the middle SUV of a trio bouncing at high speed along what appeared to be a wide dirt road but was actually the dual carriageway of the interstate highway.

These roads under the federal government care were in such severe conditions as they hadn't been appropriately maintained since the original roads had been constructed over forty years previously, and they had gotten worse in the past ten years.

The condition of the poorly maintained roads was just a symbol of the decaying national infrastructure. Doona's government had made little or no investment in the Ganuri region in the last decade.

It had been up to the regional state governors and businesses to plug the gap with limited resources.

Every now and again, the driver had to slow the vehicle down to almost a crawl so they could get through flooded gullies. The rainy season was almost at an end, but all it took was a torrential downpour to make these roads almost impassable for vehicles, which was why his fleet of cars all had four-wheel drives.

He had zero tolerance for the worthless extravagance of people he considered rich fools who had obtained their wealth through deception and corruption rather than toil and sweat and proceeded to acquire luxury items indiscriminately.

So when his security team had suggested upgrading the vehicles to include bulletproof armour as well as all-terrain capability, they'd had to make a big case for why he needed the level of protection.

Why was his life more important than the average man on the street?

"You are Zain Bassong," Samuel had replied when he'd asked that question. "You are the leader of the Movement for the Liberation of Ganuri. You did not appoint yourself to the position. We chose you to lead us because you are a man of vision, a man of strength, a man of compassion, a man of integrity.

"Yes, we know you do not want any special treatment, any special security. But we bestow it onto you because you are the ambassador and symbol of our cause. Many want you dead just as they want our cause to die. But we will do everything in our power to keep you alive and achieve our aims. When you finally leave this Earth, it will not be because we failed you. That is my prayer."

After that speech, Zain hadn't argued about any of the other upgrades to his security. The people's passion for their cause and his leadership humbled him. The least he could do was let them do their jobs just like they let him do his.

Now, he was grateful for the vehicular upgrade as they would make good time for their rendezvous.

Occasionally, they would whip past a variety of colourful local foods stacked on small tables and wooden stalls along the roadside—the yellows of pawpaw and mangos, the greens of leafy vegetables, the reds of tomatoes and chillies—the hawkers chasing after slowing cars with their wares while others sat under the shades of umbrellas.

Soon, the car turned off the highway onto an intra-state road that was in much better condition than the previous one, with the black, hardened tar still intact. It appeared the State Governor had commissioned a resurfacing project which had been completed recently.

They turned down a country lane that led them through a small town and then crested a couple of hills before turning into a tree-lined avenue with a grand, two-level mansion at the end.

At the gated entrance, security men swept the cars for explosive devices before waving them through into the large driveway. There were several cars already parked, and security and aide de camps milled around.

It seemed Zain had timed his arrival well.

One of his security men opened the back door, and he stepped out.

Canopies of enormous trees shielded the estate perched on the hilltop.

While Boma was the busy trading port and beating heart of the Ganuri region, Jaba was the soul that gave it life with its fertile lands and abundance of minerals.

A man in traditional uniform greeted Zain as he strode up the stairs. "Welcome, sir. This way, please."

He led Zain through the entrance archway and hallway into the great room.

The already seated men seemed to be deep in conversation when he entered, and they quietened.

"Your excellences," Zain said, giving a light bow before shaking hands with the three older men individually.

The youngest was about ten years older than him, and it could be argued that he had proven to be as accomplished or even more so than some of them. In Africa, people deferred to age, but that wasn't his motivation. He wanted to keep the men sweet and open to his agenda. They were the state governors of the Ganuri region, and he wanted their support.

They exchanged small talk as he asked about their families and wellbeing before taking his seat at the padded chair next to the governor of Boma State.

The retainer returned and announced, "Gani!"

All the men stood as The Gan of Ganuri, who was the traditional ruler of the Ganuri tribe, entered. He held no political status but had a powerful influence as the spiritual and ancestral leader. He wore a long, flowing white tunic that covered his feet and made him look as if he floated across the room. Vintage chunky coral beads formed a necklace around his neck and bracelets around his wrists.

He stopped by each governor and shook his hand, ending with Zain before climbing the dais and settling on the throne.

Zain and the other men sat down after him.

"Thank you for honouring my invitation," the Gan said.

There was a mixture of nods and "you're welcome."

"You are all aware of what is going on in our country, especially the Ganuri region. I have spoken to the president on these matters, and he has promised to do something. All this time, there has been no improvement. Instead, things got worse, especially with the raids on the villages. It was only when Professor Bassong stepped in and got the young men into action and defending the villages that the killings stopped. Now, those young men are protesting for their own nation. And I don't blame them."

The Governor of Jaba, the oldest of the state administrators, cleared his throat. "Your Highness, we appreciate what the young men have done with protecting the villages when the Wanai armed forces couldn't get there quick enough. But asking for a nation of Ganuri is impossible."

"Why is it impossible?" Zain asked.

"President Doona is not going to agree to break the country apart. We are part of Wanai," Governor Jaba said

"No, we are not. Not with the way the people of Ganuri are treated. Ganuri has always been independent until the colonials arrived and lumped us with Wanai as a way to subdue us after the resistance."

Ganuri had resisted colonial invasions and had fought wars against the Portuguese and the British. After Ganuri had fallen, the regional colonial administrators had merged it with the more subdued Wanai and had given Wanaians political positions over Ganuri. The power imbalance remained until today.

"That was history, and there is nothing we can do about it," Governor Jaba said.

"He is right. The president has been quite adamant about not breaking up Wanai. And we can't afford a war," Governor Boma said.

"We are already at war, living under siege like we're doing." Zain puffed out a breath. "Look, there is a simple solution to this. Let the people have their say. Give them a chance to vote in a referendum about whether they want an independent Ganuri nation or not."

"A referendum, like they did in the UK with Brexit?"

"Yes. Or Scottish Independence."

"Those referendums were flawed."

"But they were democratic. They put the power in the people's hands. We should put the options to the people of Ganuri and let then decide if they want to stay as One Wanai or not."

The men muttered to each other in low voices as they mulled over Zain's words.

Zain had thought carefully about the options available to Ganuri, and giving the people a vote would be the best way to resolve the current crisis. At least, if the majority of the people who came out to vote decided they didn't want to break from Wanai, then protesters would have to accept the results.

But first, he had an uphill struggle to convince these political administrators that it was a good thing, considering the president of Wanai was a man who had been in power for over thirty years and only allowed elections with him as the only candidate in his one-party dictatorship.

"Your Highness," the third governor, Kwamba, who hadn't said much previously, spoke up. "What do you think about the suggestion for a referendum?"

"I think we should decide by taking a vote on whether to put this out to the people of Ganuri. All those in favour of letting the people have a referendum on Ganuri Independence, raise your hand."

Zain raised his hand, and so did Governor Kwamba, which surprised him since he thought none of the governors would support the idea.

"And all those in favour of not giving the people the vote on Ganuri Independence, raise your hand."

Jaba and Boma raised their hands.

"It seems we have a draw, and I have the tiebreak," the Gan said. "I don't like the alternatives if the people feel helpless about their future. I think having a referendum is a good way to resolve this once and for all. So I'm in agreement to give the people their say in the matter."

Zain puffed out a relieved breath. He had discussed the matter with the Gan before this meeting, and the man had agreed with him. But he'd thought they would be in the minority at this table.

"Now that I have your mandate, I will call the president at the earliest opportunity and explain the decision. Hopefully, he will agree with us and allow the referendum to hold soon."

"Yes, Your Highness," the men replied.

Not long after that, Zain was back in the convoy of cars heading back to Boma. Sagging into the leather seat, he closed his eyes and allowed himself to relax for the first time in months. Certainly, the first time since he'd read about the upcoming nuptials of Isha Saene and Kweku Doona.

People talked about seeing a red mist in a state of anger.

He had seen grey ash like from a volcanic eruption.

The news had threatened to blow his life apart. For a full day, he had kept himself in seclusion, and when he had finally emerged, it had been to assemble his team and plan the abduction of the princess.

CHAPTER FOURTEEN

ISHA sat on a bench under an almond tree, looking out over the city of Boma as the sun descended in the horizon. She'd been out here for a while after she had given up on pacing her room.

Luckily, no one had stopped her from coming to sit outside. The security men who passed her occasionally as they made the tour of the perimeter said nothing to her.

After her conversation with Mrs. Bassong, she had become distraught. Even now, she couldn't accept what the woman had said about her fiancé.

She had explored other options. Could Mama have been brainwashed? In the past few years, Zain's stance on some issues had become hard-line. Would convincing his mother to tell this story be beyond him?

Then again, she hadn't known him to be deceptive. In fact, from memory, he hated any form of lies and deception, which had been part of her problem then. Zain would never tell a lie even if it was to achieve his aims.

So what was going on?

Yesterday, she'd been defending Kweku against her bodyguard who didn't entirely trust her fiancé. Today, could she defend Kweku against this accusation?

Her stomach congealed as she pictured Mama in her brokenness on a hospital bed because of the incident. If that car hadn't interrupted her descent, the injuries sustained could have been fatal.

Just like her son, Mrs. Bassong had been an activist and human rights campaigner, especially on issues surrounding equality and women. She had been outspoken, and her views were considered radical in many parts of the region. She had inspired Isha to take up advocacy until her life had taken a tragic turn.

It seemed both she and Mrs. Bassong had suffered, although differently.

The sky changed from deep orange and purple to cobalt. Spotlights provide intervals of light against the shade of the hibiscus hedges.

Beeps of car horns and shouts from the security men rent the air, followed by the clanging of metal and the rumble of car engines.

She couldn't see the driveway from her position, but she guessed it must be Zain returning home from his meeting. He'd been away for almost six hours.

The breath rushed out of her in relief. She held a smidgen of concern for his welfare even if she wouldn't admit it to his face.

She shouldn't feel anything for him. He'd ignored her for a decade.

"Do not contact me again."

She sighed and startled as a sound behind her made her turn.

"Zain," she breathed out his name.

Silhouetted by the light, without his suit jacket, the top buttons of his white shirt lay undone and showed coffee-hued skin while the cuffs were rolled up his strong arms to the elbows, revealing dark hairs.

"Sorry. I didn't mean to startle you," he said in a gentle tone.

He could dominate and reassure at the same time, a skill he'd used to massive effect in the classroom.

And the bedroom.

She coughed to clear her throat. "It's okay. I was miles away."

She couldn't admit that she'd been thinking about him.

"May I join you?" He pointed at the bench.

Why did he ask? This was his home, his garden. He could do whatever he pleased.

Instead, his voice had been gentle, enticing. Irresistible.

There was plenty of space, but she shifted to the end. "Sure."

Fabric rustled as he settled beside her. Their bodies didn't touch.

Still, her heart raced at having him so close.

She concentrated on the illumination of orange light scattered across the city of Boma like constellations.

"How did your meeting go?" She went for civil. She could do civil.

"Meeting with politicians who have their own agendas is always a so-so affair. But on the whole, the outcome seems positive."

He sighed, sounding tired as he tilted his head back.

She glanced at him. His eyes were closed, his head leaning on the trunk of the tree.

Lines fanned his eyes, and a few grey hairs mixed with the prevailing black ones.

Sitting this close to him, it became apparent how much he'd changed. How much he'd matured. Being the leader of a separatist group couldn't be easy. The responsibilities dragged a physical toll on his body, and surely on his mind, too.

Her mouth dried out, and she rubbed her palms on her dress.

"Are you okay?" she asked before she could bite her tongue.

What was wrong with her? She sounded like a woman concerned about her husband who'd come home after a hard day at work.

He opened his eyes and met her gaze.

Her breath locked in her throat. She swallowed.

"Don't worry about me. It's been a long day. That's all. What about you? Mama said you were upset earlier. She told you about the balcony incident."

"I'm fine," she said and shook her head. "No. That's a lie. I'm not fine. I've been rolling the whole thing through my mind. Kweku couldn't have pushed Mama."

Because if he did, it meant she had accepted to marry a violent man and a potential murderer. How could she live with that?

"There has to be another explanation. Maybe it really was an accident. He must have been trying to stop her from going outside, and she accidentally tipped over."

Zain sat quietly as she tried to rationalise Kweku's actions. He didn't say anything for seconds that ticked loudly in the silence like a time bomb while a vein throbbed on his temple.

After a while, he stood and took a step away. "If making up fantasies in your head makes you feel better about the man you're engaged to, well, go ahead and conjure them up. But I live in the real world. And in this world, two facts are obvious to me. Kweku Doona is responsible for Mama's fall, and you are never going to marry him."

He carried on walking towards the hedge that demarcated the courtyard from the house. On reaching the side door, he twisted the handle, pushed it, and entered the house.

Isha's anger propelled her forward. How dare he decide she wouldn't be marrying Kweku? He had no freaking right. Not after what he'd done.

"Don't you dare walk away, Zain."

She chased after him and caught him as he strode up the stairs.

"This is why you brought me here, isn't it? You don't want me to marry Kweku."

He ignored her and carried on with his journey up to the landing and into the hallway of the east wing.

She stomped after him, not caring when he entered his private suite.

"Did you abduct me just to ignore me because I'm not saying what you want me to say? Guess what? You do not have the right to dictate to me—"

He whirled around and stalked towards her, eyes gleaming.

She stepped back, and he reached across and pushed the door shut so that her back hit the slab.

"I have every right to dictate. Every right. Do I need to remind you?" he gritted out.

She swallowed and straightened her shoulders, although her heart ached. She'd spent this afternoon playing back memories she'd never wanted to rouse all because of him.

"If you're referring to what happened between us years ago, then you should know. It does not matter."

"It matters."

"No, it doesn't. Do I need to remind *you*? You ended it. You told me to abort our baby. I can never forget or forgive you for abandoning me when I needed you most."

He froze, hand hanging in the air, eyes narrowing. "Did you say baby? Were you pregnant ten years ago?"

Her chest tightened as her stomach fluttered. Her heart was shredded all over again as she remembered the trauma and her legs gave way, making her slump against the door.

"Yes. I sent you an email after you broke up with me and explained. I begged you to forgive me. Begged you to give us another chance. You sent a reply stating that you had no interest in the baby and I should abort it."

CHAPTER FIFTEEN

ZAIN'S stomach rolled, and bile rose in his throat.

There'd been a baby. They'd made a baby.

A child who'd never gotten the chance to see the world.

He turned away from Isha and rubbed his arm manically. His legs moved him towards the balcony without any thoughts of going outside. When he reached the exit, he swivelled and paced to the inner door.

Isha had slumped against it, eyes squeezed tight, her hands wrapped around her midriff in obvious distress.

Ache bloomed in his chest, joining the hurt in the back of his pharynx.

He should hold her and make everything well again for her.

Still, he couldn't bring himself to touch her.

She had aborted their baby.

How could she ever think that he wouldn't want his offspring? His blood.

He growled in anguish, bent over, and gripped his head. "Isha, how could you?"

A sob fell from her.

He lifted his head to find tears seeping from her closed eyes. "You aborted our baby."

"What?" Her eyelids fluttered, and she stared at him incredulously. "I did no such thing!"

She swiped at the tears on her cheeks with the back of her hand.

Hope bloomed in his chest. "What are you saying? We have a child?"

Another sob left her. And yet another. As if a dam had burst inside her, every time she opened her mouth, a cry came out.

Unable to stop himself, he straightened, scooped her up, and strode over to the divan. He sat on the edge, with her on his lap.

"I tried to keep our baby. I thought if I didn't tell anyone until it was past a certain time, then my parents would have to let me keep the pregnancy," she said between sobs. "Then I got ill and ended up in the emergency room. By the time I woke up, there was no baby. Apparently, they'd had to terminate, or I would have died."

His mind went in a spin. His heart hurt, and he had difficulty swallowing. He wanted to rage at all that he had lost. Yet, he constrained his anguish and focused on the distraught woman in his arms.

He closed his eyes and pulled her even closer.

Her chest heaved, and her body trembled.

Outside, an owl's cry echoed while warm air fluttered the light curtain at the window.

At this moment, he wasn't the professor influencing young minds, or the lawyer fighting for justice, or the activist fighting for human rights, or a separatist seeking freedom for his people. Those roles came with rigid rules and boundaries. Duty, strength, and composure.

For the first time in years, he was simply a man. Zain.

This woman did it to him. She freed the person he kept private and locked away when he had to be all those things for all those people.

With her, he became unconstrained, and once upon a time, he'd been vulnerable with her.

He hadn't turned on the light when he'd come in. First, they had been lit with the bulb from the corridor. Now, with the door shut, the moonlight cast silver beams into the room. Downstairs, there was a brief murmur of conversation.

Unease made his back prickle.

When he'd taken Isha and brought her to his house, the plan had been simple—get her to convince Doona to give Ganuri the referendum.

He hadn't trusted her because of her past deception.

Was she deceiving him now about the baby?

No. Her distress was real.

And he wanted to trust that there had been something genuine about their relationship all those years ago, although she had lied about her status and background.

Things had become complicated.

Knowing what she'd been through all those years ago, finding out she'd been pregnant and alone and had lost their baby, he had to think of another way.

Although Doona and his ilk might want to brand him as evil, he had never knowingly chosen to hurt anyone.

Abducting Isha had been wrong, but his intention had not been to hurt her.

After a while, her sobs quietened, replaced by the sound of her regular breathing. She had fallen asleep.

He stretched her out on the bed and took her shoes off. She remained fully clothed. He didn't bother to remove those. He'd already taken liberties. He wouldn't take any more.

He covered her up, gave her one last look, and left the room. With slow and heavy strides, he went down the corridor to his mother's quarters, which was at the end of the hall. Taking a deep breath, he knocked on the door.

"Come in," the female voice came through.

He twisted the handle and opened the door. His mother sat in the armchair reading a book in the lamplight, her spectacles perched on her nose. She looked up when he walked in.

"Son, what's the matter?" She must have seen his grave expression.

He shut the door and slumped against it as he sucked in a deep breath.

"Mama, did Ruby—Isha tell you about our baby?"

His mother's eyes went wide. She removed her spectacles and placed it along with the book on the table. "Baby? No. She had a baby?"

"She carried him ... her." He didn't even know the gender. A lump lodged in his throat, making him croak. He swallowed with difficulty. "She lost the baby after a few months."

"Almighty!" his mother cried out and clasped her working hand over her mouth. Her eyes shone with unshed tears.

His eyes misted.

"Oh, son." She spread her arm. "I'm so sorry."

He stumbled forward and allowed his mother to embrace him.

She'd known all those years ago when he'd fallen in love with Isha. He'd called her and confessed his love for a girl he'd met in London, which had prompted his mother to visit him there so she could see the woman who had claimed her son's heart.

When he'd broken things off with Isha after he'd found out her true identity, his mother had been there afterwards. Although he'd never appropriately grieved since he'd attempted to shove Isha out of his mind until the day he'd seen her photograph standing alongside Kweku Doona as they announced their engagement.

Grieving a lover who had deceived you was one thing. Grieving an infant? His blood?

His heart wrenched, the pain spreading to his limbs.

"I should have been there with her." Maybe if he hadn't ended things with Isha, the pregnancy would have gone full term, and they would have a nine-year-old child running around.

"You didn't know," his mother said.

He leaned back and straightened. He blamed himself, regardless. "I should have realised that she could've been pregnant. I should have waited a little longer before breaking off the relationship. But I was angry with her. I thought she was one of those young people who liked to play games. She had lied about the most basic things about her and had gone to an effort to cover them up. I thought she'd faked the rest."

Some students liked to be able to manipulate their lecturers, just like there were professors who abused their positions over students.

"There are some things that cannot be faked, son. Remember, I met her. Yes, she lied. Still, I saw a girl in love with you."

"It doesn't make it right."

"No, it doesn't. But why didn't she tell you that she was pregnant?"

"She said she sent me an email, but I never got any emails from her after we broke up."

"Do you think she's lying again?"

"I don't know. I don't think so. She appeared genuinely distraught and broke down when she told me. Why would she lie now when I know the rest?"

His mother sighed. "From the timelines, it seems it must have happened while I was in the hospital after the balcony incident. And afterwards, you were arrested and detained. Didn't you say that you think one of your email accounts was hacked, which was why you deactivated it?"

He staggered backwards as it hit him.

"Yes. That's it. Doona's secret police hacked into my email account. They must have seen her email." His stomach rolled again. "She said that she got a reply from me telling her that I didn't care about the baby and she should abort it."

"Goodness!" Mama gasped.

"I would never disown my own blood or wipe out its existence," he bit out angrily.

"I know that, son."

"All this while, she thought that I didn't want my child."

"Doona has taken so much from our family."

"We have sacrificed so much for our people. Isha has made sacrifices, too, although unwittingly. How can I justify keeping her here against her will? Yet, if I let her go without accomplishing our goals, then all those sacrifices have been in vain, and the Doonas will win again."

This was the dilemma now tearing him apart. Stuck between fulfilling his promise to his people and setting the woman he loved free.

CHAPTER SIXTEEN

ISHA woke with a start. The room was strange until she remembered yesterday, waking up and finding out she'd been abducted from a party and was now being held in Zain's house.

But this wasn't the room she'd been assigned.

This one was intensely masculine with the dark wood furniture, leather settee, and huge bed.

Zain's room. Angry last night, she'd followed him in here and had ended up telling him how she'd lost her pregnancy years ago.

She must have fallen asleep in his arms, and he'd let her stay here all night. She still wore her clothes without her sandals.

A knock on the door had her sitting up. "Come."

Zain strode in wearing navy jeans and a grey T-shirt and carrying a tray. "Good morning, Princess."

"Good morning, Zain."

She swung her feet over the edge and stood, her heart thumping. Last night, she'd allowed herself to be vulnerable in front of him, in front of anyone, for the first time in years. She had to get out of here.

"I'll just get my sandals and get out of your room."

"No. Stay." He placed the tray on the low table in front of the leather sofa.

"I can't." She bent to pick up her shoes.

"Please," he said in a hoarse voice.

She raised her head, mouth flying open. Hadn't he been the one making demands yesterday? What had changed? Was it because she'd broken down in tears? Did he pity her?

She stiffened her spine as her eyes narrowed. "Why do you want me to stay?"

"I was hoping we could share breakfast and talk."

"Share breakfast? What are we? Friends?" She raised her hand in a stop gesture. "If this is about last night and you're feeling pity for me because of what I told you, just forget it. I don't want your pity."

She didn't want anyone's pity.

She marched towards the exit on bare feet.

Zain intercepted her. "After last night, I feel a lot of things, but pity is not one of them. I just want to call a truce."

"A truce?"

"Yes. So we can talk. Will you join me for breakfast?" He waved at the sofa.

"Sure. But I'd like to use the bathroom first."

He pointed at a closed door. "My bathroom is through there."

She dropped her sandals and walked to the door, closing it behind her.

In the mirror, she looked rumpled—creased dress, curls of hair loose from her ponytail, and cheeks that still had tracks from her last night's tears.

She splashed water on her face and found a clean towel to pat it dry, and then she rinsed out her mouth before brushing back her hair with her palm and rebinding the ponytail. There was nothing she could do about the dress until she got back to her room.

Her room? It wasn't her room. It was just the space she'd been assigned while she remained a Zain's prisoner.

But he'd called a truce, and now, she would have breakfast with him like civilised people.

Like a couple.

Don't go there.

Anyway, the dress would have to do as is.

Not like he hadn't seen her in worse.

Not like he hadn't seen her naked.

Don't go there!

She squeezed her eyes shut and sucked in a deep breath.

When she opened her lids, she headed into the bedroom.

Zain stood by the door leading to the balcony with his hands in his pockets, and his expressionless gaze followed her as she settled on the sofa. He pulled the armchair, so it was close to the low table, and sat down. Then, he opened the covered dishes—grapefruit segments, boiled plantains, and egg stew.

Her stomach rumbled, and her mouth watered. She hadn't eaten since lunch. The staff had offered her dinner while Zain had been out yesterday, but she had refused.

She took a plate and helped herself to the plantain and egg stew.

"Did you make these?"

She couldn't stop herself. He used to make the breakfast meal for her years ago after she'd spend the night at his. Now, he had domestic staff, so he probably didn't go into the kitchen. "Sorry."

"No need to be sorry," he said as he picked up another plate. "I made breakfast as an olive branch. To show you that I don't want to fight you."

She swallowed the piece of plantain in her mouth.

"So if you don't want to fight me, your tactic is to seduce me?" she asked almost flippantly.

She couldn't forget what he'd said about her never marrying Kweku.

He grimaced before his gaze swept over her body, heating it up in the process. "I will admit that I find you extremely attractive. Have always done. Contrary to what you think, I did not bring you here to seduce you or as some kind of vendetta against your fiancé."

His jaw tightened briefly.

"So why did you bring me here?"

"You are here because I need to save my people."

"Save your people? That's a little dramatic, don't you think?"

"Dramatic? Perhaps. True? Absolutely."

"So how am I supposed to save your people?"

"I want you to convince President Doona to agree to a referendum on Ganuri Independence."

"What? I can't do that. I don't have that kind of influence on the president."

"But your father does. And you have influence over your fiancé, don't you?"

"Well, yes," she hesitated.

"And Kweku is set to take over from his father once he gets married."

"Yes."

"So you can convince him that letting the people vote on their future will be a great way to start his presidency."

"Yes, that's true. But why would I want to do any of that?"

"Because in exchange for you helping my people, I will let you go home, and I won't disturb you again."

"When I go home, I am set to marry Kweku. You'd let that happen?"

"Yes. I don't like Kweku Doona, or any other Doonas, for that matter. But if he is the man you love and the one you've chosen to spend the rest of your life with, then I will let you go and wish you the best."

This was indeed a different man from the one telling her she would never marry Kweku.

But ...

"I have to ask you. Why do you want independence so much?"

He tilted his head and stared at her. "I can tell you a million reasons why Ganuri deserves to be its own nation. But I would prefer to show you. Will you let me show you what I am fighting for, Princess?"

CHAPTER SEVENTEEN

THE sun had risen high in the sky before Zain had stopped enough to think again about his conversation with Isha this morning and their upcoming trip.

He'd spent the past few hours with his team, going over contingency plans to tackle military invasion in the Ganuri region and failure to secure the referendum vote.

For the first time since Isha's arrival, a sizzle of anticipation had flown through him, and he'd struggled not to grin all morning.

He'd finally managed to have a conversation with her without arguments or tension between them. She'd agreed to travel through Ganuri with him so he could show her all the things that the Doonas didn't want the rest of the world to see since they had prohibited journalists and restricted Internet access to his people.

In truth, he looked forward to spending time with Isha more than anything else.

He'd thought ten years without her would have cleansed her from his system.

The reverse seemed to be the case.

He wanted her now more than he'd thought possible.

But she remained engaged to another man. She hadn't denied that she loved Kweku when he'd mentioned it.

It hurt to know that she was in love with another man that wasn't him.

However, it wasn't surprising considering she must have hated him when she'd thought he'd sent a nasty email to her rejecting their baby.

A bolt of anger went through him, and he shoved it aside.

He wouldn't allow Doona to taint the small victory he'd achieved today by getting Isha to stay in Ganuri willingly.

And he couldn't forget the fact that she had responded to his kiss yesterday.

Despite her anger at him, she felt something. Perhaps not love. But desire.

The same all-consuming attraction that had drawn them together ten years ago simmered whenever they were in the same room.

He hungered for her. He couldn't deny it.

Before their time together ended, he wanted a chance to assuage that craving.

He strode down the hall towards her bedroom. He'd instructed her to pack for the trip. They'd be away for at least a week.

How would she cope without a personal maid to do the chores for her?

He knocked on the door.

It swung open, and she stood on the other side dressed in a pair of dark blue denim jeans and black T-shirt, her hair styled in a chignon.

His breath caught in his throat.

Looking young and stylish, like she'd been a decade ago when he'd first met her, beautiful and stunning.

Perfect cinnamon skin bare of makeup, full black lashes fluttering over high cheekbones, this was the woman he'd fallen in love with, the intelligent, argumentative woman who seemed down to earth and yet had the spirit of a crusader.

His heart rattled. The old feelings came rushing back.

His body reacted, hardening, and his mouth watered for a taste of her heart-shaped lips.

The past few years, he'd been too busy for women, focusing his energies on his enormous responsibilities.

He had to admit it to himself. He hadn't been too busy. He'd only craved one woman. The one standing right in front of him.

He'd promised that he would let her go home and not bother her again.

But staring at her now, he didn't even want to let her out of his sight.

"Zain?" She looked up at him, her expression concerned.

He blinked several times and cleared his throat. "Are you ready to go?"

"Yes." She pulled a small suitcase from the corner and dragged it to the door.

"I'll take it for you." He reached for the handle and lifted the light luggage.

"Thank you."

She sounded sober as if she had thoughts disturbing her, too.

He carried the suitcase down the stairs where a servant took it from him.

Mama and Aliyah waited in the living room.

"We're heading out now," he said as he leaned down to embrace his mother. "Latifah will be here in an hour or so. I spoke to her this morning."

"That's great. I was beginning to worry about her," Mrs. Bassong replied.

"You shouldn't worry about her." He glanced back at his mother as he strode over to Aliyah.

"I worry about all my children," Mama replied and turned her attention to Isha. "And that includes you. Be safe out there."

"I'm sure we'll be fine, Mama." Isha hugged his mother.

"We will be," he said as he pressed his lips to Aliyah's temple. "I'm more concerned about leaving the two of you at such an unstable period. But Solomon is staying behind until Latifah arrives."

In the past decade, he had refused to be away from his mother for more than a few days at a time after the disastrous visit from the Wanai Secret Police.

He'd given up his position as a visiting lecturer and hadn't accepted any other offers that involving being away for several weeks. His mother refused to leave her homeland and go into exile. Neither would he.

Samuel came to the door. "We have to get going."

"Bye, Mama," Isha said as she headed for the exit.

"Have a safe trip," his mother replied.

"We'll see you in a few days," Zain said.

Outside stood the blacked-out SUVs of the motorcade. The security team and servants bustled around the three vehicles, storing luggage and other equipment.

He glanced at Isha, wishing he could whisk her away on a private trip with just the two of them.

Impossible.

Still a member of a royal family, she had to be kept safe. He needed to ensure her security.

She didn't say anything as the chauffeur held the door. She sashayed past him, avoiding any physical contact and slid into the backseat.

He got in to find her at the farthest end away from him. She didn't look at him or even acknowledge his presence.

Hadn't they broken the ice already?

What had changed between this morning and now? Had she changed her mind about travelling with him? Had she pretended to go along with plans for the trip?

It wouldn't be the first time she had deceived him.

Memories shimmered in his mind, threatening to darken his mood. He shoved it aside.

This trip wasn't about the past. He focused on the future.

The future of the people of Ganuri.

As long as he kept the objective in mind, everything else should be easy to handle.

The convoy moved swiftly through the city aided by the outriders on bikes with sirens clearing the roads. They turned off onto the intra-state highway.

Isha still refused to look at him or talk to him. Her stony gaze remained fixed outside the speeding vehicle and whizzing scenery—green fields, trees, and the occasional small town.

Two hours after they'd left the city, they slowed at the approach to a fork on the road and took the left turn. Soon, they pulled up on the dusty field outside a school building. The security men opened the doors for them.

Zain stepped out and strode over to Isha.

A man in a short-sleeved white shirt and brown trousers approached them with a smile.

"Welcome, Professor Bassong. It is good to have you visit us today." The man extended his hand as he bowed.

"Thank you for taking the time for us at such short notice, Principal Korli." Zain shook the man's hand. "This is Ms. Saene. She is here as an independent international observer to see how the community has coped since the attack and what can be done to help."

He turned to Isha, who glanced at him with an unreadable expression.

"Principal Korli, it's nice to meet you," she said and reached out to take the man's hand.

"You are welcome, Ms. Saene. If you will follow me, please." Principal Korli led the way into the building. "This is the administrative block with the staff offices. My office is this way."

"I noticed some holes in the wall outside. Can you tell me what happened here?" Isha asked.

Zain's breath stalled, and blood rushed in his ears. He struggled not to grin like a fool.

It would be easy for the ordinary eye to miss those marks, to assume that the school was old and rundown, perhaps, and miss the actual truth.

For someone of Isha's stature, this environment and everything within it would be beneath her. People of her class didn't visit schools like this. And if they were ever to make a trip to a more impoverished neighbourhood, it would be to launch a spanking new facility, with a troupe of people singing their praises and cameramen for photo opportunities.

There was no dancing troupes or media circus here.

Yet, Isha had noticed.

How could he have forgotten how observant she'd proven to be so many years ago?

And she seemed totally at ease here.

Korli glanced at Zain and then back at Isha. "I'm sorry. I didn't realise you didn't know about the attack."

"I didn't want to influence Ms. Saene's opinion of the event until she had seen the place and spoken to survivors," Zain explained.

"Of course. That is understandable." Korli waved his hand towards the exit. "Three months ago, the school came under attack by unknown gunmen. They shot at the staff and were going to abduct our students. Luckily, the local vigilante group came to our rescue. They fought the attackers and saved our students. Unfortunately, two members of staff died, and some of the vigilante group were injured. The holes in the walls were made by the bullets. Now, we have armed guards patrolling the grounds during the school day to make sure the attack doesn't happen again."

Chapter Eighteen

ISHA tapped her fingers on the armrest, and her foot bounced against floor mat. Her chest grew tight, and her throat closed up. She rocked back and forth.

"Princess, are you okay?"

Zain's voice seemed to come from miles away in the enclosed space of the vehicle.

"No. I'm not okay," she said in a strained voice. "Let me out."

"Stop the car," he ordered.

"Prof, this area is not secure," Samuel replied from the front passenger seat.

"Then secure it. She's not feeling well."

"Sure." Samuel lifted his hand and pressed a button on his headset. "We're stopping here. Everyone on alert."

The car pulled to a stop. Samuel came out and opened the back door.

Isha unclipped her seat belt and jumped out. After the freezing temperature of the car AC, the night air hit her like a hot wall.

She bent over and sucked in oxygen, taking gulps at a time.

These past four days had been intense. From the first trip to the school that had come under attack, it had been non-stop.

She had met students and teachers who had survived the attack, courageous people in her opinion, considering many had refused to return to the school after the incident.

Yesterday, they had visited yet another village that had come under attack. One of the first places, where thirty had been killed, and girls had been raped, not to mention the many injured.

Today, they had visited one of the many camps for Internally Displaced People.

People who had lost family, friends, and properties in unprovoked armed attacks.

People who were too afraid to go back to their homes for fear of more attacks.

People living in tents in what was quickly turning into slums with no running water or other amenities.

They were citizens of Wanai. And yet, refugees in their own country. Men. Women, Children. Young. Old.

Now, her head was full of the images.

Someone rubbed a palm between her shoulder blades, drawing her from her thoughts, trying to soothe her. She didn't need to look up to know that it was Zain.

She straightened.

"What is going on around here? How have all these things happened?" She jerked her fingers in the direction they had come from. The IDP camp was about an hour's drive back there. "I've seen graves and grieving families and shot-up schools, for goodness' sake, and yet, none of that was in the news."

The headlights of the third SUV illuminated Zain. He had his hands in his trouser pockets. "Doona won't allow any of it to get out. He controls most of the news outlets, and even those he doesn't control will not report anything he doesn't approve. He cut off Internet access for the region, and the last foreign journalists that tried getting into Ganuri got abducted. One got killed, and the others supposedly were rescued and returned home. Of course, the world lets him get away with anything he likes because he calls us terrorists."

Isha grimaced. She had been one of those people who had labelled the MLG group as terrorists unjustly and without knowing all the facts.

So far, all she had seen were people who were trying to live their lives under difficult circumstances. Everyone seemed to have praise for Zain. Their respect for him showed in the way they looked up to him. He had done everything he could to keep the people of Ganuri safe since the government seemed to be failing in that aspect.

What was so wrong with the people choosing how they wanted to be governed?

But it didn't make sense. None of it did.

"So who are the armed men raiding the towns? Has any of them being caught or tried?" Her frustration seeped into her voice.

"In the past, the army or police never arrived in time to apprehend any of the assailants. When we organised the vigilantes, they killed some of the attackers, but none was ever taken alive. They seemed too organised. We think they are military, and the attacks are ordered by Doona as part of his siege against Ganuri and the MLG."

She shook her head and gritted her teeth. "Attacking his citizens? What a bad strategy. If I were the MLG, I wouldn't back down. I would fight back."

The words had come out of her mouth before she realised what she'd said.

Zain moved close, his gaze intense as he placed his hands on her shoulders. "You said it."

She lifted her hands and scrubbed her face. "Look, I'm not advocating for war."

"Neither am I. That's why you're here, remember?" He squeezed her shoulders. "It has been four long, exhausting days, and we're all tired. Why don't we head to the hotel? It might not be exactly what you're used to, but it's nice and clean, and we can even take tomorrow off so you can have some time to rest and recharge. How does that sound?"

"Sounds good." She could do with a shower and fresh, clean sheets. Hopefully, she would sleep better tonight than the last three nights.

He guided her back to the car where one of the bodyguards held the door.

Thirty minutes later, they pulled up outside the bright lights of a hotel lobby. Zain and Isha were ushered straight to their suite. The security team did a sweep of the place before leaving them to it. It had separate bedrooms connected by a living area with mink-upholstered settees and teakwood furniture.

"This is nice," Isha said as she opened the door to one of the bedrooms.

"Yes. It's their king suite." Zain stood behind her.

She glanced back with her eyebrow raised. "King suite?"

He shrugged and grinned. "The very best."

He had such a sexy grin, and she couldn't help a returning smile. "As long as the water is hot and the sheets are fresh, I'm happy. I'm off to the shower."

"I'm going to order some food. Is there anything you want, especially?"

"I'm not massively hungry. So just order whatever."

A knock on the door distracted Zain.

Isha took the opportunity to head to the bathroom. She turned on the shower, stripped down, and stepped into the cubicle. Warm water cascaded onto her skin, and she let out a sigh of pleasure.

"Isha." Zain's voice came from the bedroom.

Her heart raced. Would he come into the bathroom? She hadn't shut the door completely.

"Yes?" Her voice sounded croaky.

"I brought your baggage," he said.

She gulped. "Oh. Thank you."

"You're welcome. See you later." His footsteps faded.

She let out a frustrated sigh and pressed her forehead against the tiles.

Why was she disappointed that Zain hadn't come into the bathroom? Since the time he'd kissed her six days ago, he hadn't done anything remotely suggestive. Not even when she'd spent the night in his bed.

It seemed he would keep to his promise of letting her go so she could marry Kweku.

Kweku. She had thought less and less of him in the past days. The only time she remembered him concerned Mama's fall from the balcony.

And yet, she thought about Zain, almost nonstop.

Granted, she interacted with him every day.

But shouldn't absence make the heart grow fonder in Kweku's case?

Shouldn't she be pining for him instead of wishing for Zain to walk into the bathroom and find her naked? Instead of wanting Zain to strip off his clothes and join her in the shower like he'd done all those years ago?

The same Zain who had broken off their affair and told her never to contact him again. The one who'd told her he didn't want anything to do with their baby. Never mind that he behaved as if he hadn't known about the child until a few days ago. He could be pretending.

The same Zain who had abducted her and held her captive for his own aims. Not to mention that he could be married to Aliyah.

What was wrong with her?

What was this irresistible urge to reconnect with him?

Why had she even agreed to help him?

The crusader in her couldn't stand back and watch innocent civilians being persecuted by their government.

Still, she should be thinking of getting away from him, going home and back to her life without him. The hotel would have phones, so she could call home to send for rescue.

That's what she would do. She would wait until Zain had settled for the night and make the call. Hopefully, her family's security team would be here before daybreak.

Decision made, she switched off the faucet, stepped out of the cubicle, grabbed the white hotel robe, and wrapped it around her body.

If everything went right, she wouldn't see Zain again after tonight.

Her heart ached, and she rubbed her chest.

She shoved the feeling aside and went into the bedroom, dug into her luggage, and found the detangling hairbrush she'd packed. Then, she returned to the bathroom and blow-dried her hair until it was straight and sleek.

A sound made her look up. Zain stood at the bathroom door in a white T-shirt, cargo shorts, and bare feet. His cropped hair had drops of water. He must have just had a shower, too.

Her breath caught as he watched her with a serious expression. She switched off the dryer and placed it back on the hook.

"I didn't want to disturb you, but dinner is here, and I thought you wouldn't want it cold," he said.

"Thanks. I'll just put something on."

"Sure." He backed off.

She returned to the bedroom and found a black and white, cotton T-shirt and shorts night set which came with a short robe. Dressed, she entered the living room.

Zain stood by the dining area, chatting on a cordless phone. He ended the conversation as she approached the table.

The phone reminded her of her resolve to call home tonight.

The back of her throat hurt, and she tugged the sash of her robe tight.

Zain strode over and pulled out a chair.

His heat caressed her back, and his scent filled her nostrils. A memory tugged of the first time he'd cooked dinner for her in his apartment.

He'd pulled the chair out for her that night and brushed her cheek with his lips after she'd settled.

"Thank you." Her voice was almost a whisper. Her heart rate increased as she lowered her body onto the cushioned seat.

Would he kiss her cheek?

He didn't and walked over to the other side. "You're welcome."

She lowered her head as her chest tightened.

Why was she disappointed that he hadn't caressed her skin? Why was she so hung up on him?

"Are you feeling better now?" he said from where he sat across the table.

"Yes." That was a lie, and she'd sworn to herself she wouldn't lie to him again. "No. I'm not feeling better." She pushed back the chair and stood. "You should have brought Aliyah with you. You should be sitting with her and having this meal."

Then, she wouldn't have to deal with the temptation he provided if there was another woman physically between them.

His brows furrowed. "Aliyah? What are you talking about?"

"Is she not your girlfriend?" She balled her hands on the table.

He grimaced. "She's not my girlfriend."

"Wife, then?"

He pushed his chair back and straightened. "Aliyah is not my girlfriend, wife, fiancée, mistress, or anything else. She is my adoptive sister. She was rescued from a people-smuggling ring as a teenager, and Mama adopted her."

He strode around the table and stopped at the edge. The air vibrated with the tension of their attraction. His dark gaze pinned her and held her captive.

"If you're not with Aliyah or anyone else, then it means you haven't forgiven me for what happened years ago." She kept her gaze averted.

"Why should it matter if I've forgiven you or not? You are engaged to another man. Every time I see you, his ring glitters on your finger. And worse, you think I'm a terrorist."

His voice was sharp and cut through her.

Her cheeks burned, and she crumpled into the chair as her shame returned.

The shame of wanting a different man from the one she had agreed to marry.

The old shame of being caught out on a lie by the man she loved.

"Forget I said anything." She sucked in a huge breath.

"No. You opened this door. We have unresolved matters, and this is as good a time to trash them out." He came close, close enough to touch.

Her heart raced, and she clenched her palms on her lap. She had nothing to say without confessing that no matter how much she had tried to hate him over the past decade, she had never been able to scrub away her true feelings for him.

Chapter Nineteen

ZAIN had prepared himself for everything. Or so he had thought. He'd focused himself on the ultimate objective—Ganuri referendum.

The plan had been to take Isha on this road trip and show her all the horrors of Doona's making, in a bid to appeal to the crusader in her.

Once they had shown her the exact situation of his people, she would use her advocacy skills to persuade her father and eventually President Doona to allow his people their vote.

And then, she would be gone from his life.

He swivelled and walked to the far wall, hands balled into fists. His skin overheated.

With a few sentences, she had lit a keg of gunpowder inside him, exploding his emotions out of his control.

He'd thought he could let her go without confronting what happened in the past. He'd thought wrong.

The anger and betrayal he'd felt returned.

He rubbed the back of his clammy neck and faced her.

She sat crouched on the chair, her gaze averted, her arms crossed over her stomach.

She looked nothing like the imperious and obstinate princess he'd encountered six days ago.

Something tugged at him. He should care. He should scoop her up, make every problem go away.

He shook his head. He couldn't touch her again without stripping her and claiming what was rightfully his, and where would that get them?

In any case, he shouldn't care. Shouldn't feel anything for her.

He should dish out the wickedness she seemed to think he could exhibit when she had labelled him a terrorist. He should let her feel every bit of hurt and heartbreak and misery he had undergone because of her.

"I cared about you," he said in a low voice. "More than I've ever cared about another woman before or since."

She heaved a breath and nodded as if unable to speak. Her body trembled.

"I fell in love with you from that first day you spoke up in my class," he continued. "I can never forget your words when I asked the question about The Four Horsemen of the Apocalypse. If I close my eyes, I can still remember what you were wearing and where you sat in the lecture hall. None of the other students had raised their hands. Yours was the lone arm up in the air, still and composed. Do you recall your answer, Isha?"

Her head bobbed in an agitated motion, and her throat rippled. She looked up at him. Her eyes shimmered with the light. "War is the most avoidable of the four."

"The exact same words. And the passion in your voice when you defended your statement to the class. I hadn't heard any other student speak with such zeal about a subject. Falling in love with you after that seemed inevitable. For months, I resisted. I'm not a man given to impulsive behaviour. I had never ever looked at any of my students as more than just students until you came along."

He strode towards her in slow, deliberate motions.

"You were my one and only. I wanted to cherish you, to love and protect you forever," he said when he stopped at the table beside her.

"I'm sorry." Tears dropped from her lashes onto her cheeks, and a tremor chased over her.

He glanced away, unable to look at her without crumbling and reaching for her.

With the rest of the world, he could be the stern professor or an aggressive activist.

With Isha, he became unguarded. Just a man who loved a woman.

All those years ago, he'd prepared for a future where he would fight his battles with her by his side. He had been taken unawares to find that she stood on the opposite of the divide, one of the people he would battle.

"I bared my soul to you, and yet, you couldn't tell me the truth about yourself. I was just a fling to you."

"No. It wasn't like that." She swiped her face.

"Don't lie to me, Isha. I know that your family would have never approved of me. They had chosen other more suitable suitors."

"I'm not lying."

She raised her hand towards him.

He did nothing to bridge the gap.

She let it fall back onto her lap. "Yes. When we started seeing each other, I had thought that I would have to give you up in the end. So I thought it best not to tell you my true identity. And by the time I summoned the courage to tell you the truth, it was too late. There had been too many lies. I just didn't know how to confess. And then, when we discussed making the trip to Boma, I told you that I wanted us to visit Bagumi, too. I was going to show you my true identity. But you had to travel to Wanai on an emergency, and then, you found out the truth somehow, and everything changed."

"You were dating Kweku at the same time as you dated me," he bit out angrily.

"No. No. He is my brother Zawadi's friend. We hung out occasionally, but I only started dating him properly a few years ago."

"Tell the fucking truth, Isha. You went on dates with him ten years ago."

"No. Once when he came to London, he asked me on a date. But that was the night we got together. Remember, I told you I had a date, and I sent him a text to cancel. Afterwards, I only ever hung out with him when my brothers were around."

She stood and stumbled in his direction. "I swear to you on my life, Zain. I'm telling you the truth."

Something broke inside him. He stretched his arms. One hand grasped her nape, the other her waist.

Her palms settled on his chest. Her body trembled as she looked up at him with pleading eyes.

His heart cracked. He tightened his jaw.

This wasn't the time to give in. He needed to finish what they had started. They needed closure.

"And then what?" he ground out.

She blinked several times and looked at him in confusion. "What do you mean?"

"Let's assume you had taken me to Bagumi to meet your parents, and they told me to get out of their palace, that I wasn't suitable for you. What would you have done then?"

Her brows furrowed as she raised her chin and gripped his shirt in a fist. "I would have told them that you were my chosen one. I would have told them that you were my heart. I would have fought for you anyway I could to keep you. But you gave up on our baby and me. You didn't even give us a chance."

His anger dissipated as soon as she mentioned 'baby.'

If only he could go back and change things.

"Isha, I swear to you on everything I hold dear, I didn't know that you were pregnant until last week."

She gave him an incredulous stare as her fingers touched her lips. "You sent me an email."

"That email wasn't from me." His fingers and thumb gripped her jaw. "I would never tell you or anyone else to abort my child."

"But if it wasn't from you ..." she trailed off as if unable to finish the question.

"Someone else sent the message. My email account was hacked. I had to deactivate the account when I found out."

"Oh, Lord." Fresh tears beaded her black lashes. "You didn't know about our baby, and all this time, I hated you for something you didn't do." She shoved at his chest. "This just gets worse and worse."

"No, it doesn't." He kept his grip on her. "It wasn't your fault."

"I deceived you. That's what started it all."

"Maybe. But I should have realised you could be pregnant. I should have been with you. If I'd been there, maybe our baby would have lived."

He scrubbed his hand over his face and head as the back of his throat hurt, and his anguish returned.

"I should have been there with you." His voice choked, and he struggled to swallow as his eyes misted. "I'm sorry that I failed you."

He closed his eyes. His chest hurt, and he struggled to breathe.

Fingers curled around his neck and tugged his head down. He opened his eyes as she pressed her lips against the tear on his cheek.

"Forgive yourself. Forgive me. Wipe the slate clean." Her warm breath whispered against his flesh, sensitising it.

It took a few seconds for her words and their meaning to register.

He stilled, searching her face. "There's only one way to do that, Isha? Are you sure?"

"I'm sure. Please, I need it. I need you."

She hovered close to the edge, and the only thing he could do was to breach the gap between them. Mouth to mouth, body to body.

As soon as he touched her soft lips in the hard kiss, he wanted more. More of her. More of everything that he had missed out on over the past decade. Her body, her heart. Her soul.

He kissed her as if his life depended on it. Once upon a time, he would have given his life for her. He still could offer his life to her.

She yielded, her body going pliant in his arms as she pressed against him. He sucked the tip of her tongue, tasting the sweetness of her mouth as well as the promise of more.

He stroked her breasts through her T-shirt, and she moaned. She wore no bra, and the nipples hardened against his palm.

He growled, lifted her waist as she wrapped her legs around his hips.

"I forgive you for everything, Isha. But you're going to have to forgive me for what I'm about to do."

He carried her towards the bedroom. He'd given up on fighting the inferno of desire that had exploded inside him.

"What?" she asked, her breath whispering on the skin of his neck as she clung on to him.

"I'm going to make love to you."

He paused at the wall separating his room from the lounge. Body plastered to hers, he pushed her against the concrete and leaned his head against hers.

"Unless you don't want me to. Tell me you don't want me, and I'll stop, and we can go back to the cold dinner."

PART THREE

IN LOVE

CHAPTER TWENTY

ISHA'S breath came in choppy pants. What was she doing?

One minute, they had been having an intense conversation about the past which she'd inadvertently triggered by talking about his relationship with Aliyah.

He'd flayed her when he'd described his love and commitment to her until he'd found out about her deceptions.

She'd lobbed the accusation about his abandonment of her and their baby.

Finding out he hadn't sent the awful email had depressed her. She'd had no more comebacks. No defence.

However, the distress in his voice and the teardrop on his skin had had her chest squeezing tight. Without thinking, she'd stood on the tips of her toes and pressed her mouth to the spot. She had wanted to soothe him, to take away his despair.

Everything had changed with the caress.

He'd taken over. Of course he'd taken over. It was in his nature to lead. To control.

She had become lost in the strength of his kiss, the firmness of his lips, and the roughness of his beard.

A fever had spread through her, the same one bubbling in her veins. Like a volcanic eruption, her desire for him flowed out and extinguished any resistance she might have.

He held her against the wall as if this was the last checkpoint, the final line of separation. When they crossed into his room, there would be no past or future, just the here and now.

She tugged the engagement ring from her finger and tossed it on the sideboard which stood against the wall.

"I can't tell you to stop because I want you to make love to me," she whispered against his mouth, finally revealing her pent-up craving for him.

She had never stopped craving him.

With a growl, he manoeuvred them through the door, and her next awareness was of her body spread over his lap on the bed, her hands braced on the carpeted floor while legs were on the other side.

"You have been a bad girl, Ruby," he said in a husky voice as he stroked his palm down her back.

With those words, she went back ten years to the innocent girl he'd taken in hand for her unruly behaviour in the night club. Her skin tingled, and her pulse sky-rocketed.

"I'm sorry, Sir," she whispered in a hoarse voice.

"I know you are, Ruby, but a naughty girl gets punished."

She tensed as a smack landed on her left bottom. "Ah."

Jolting, she tried to anticipate the next one, but it was still a shock as he didn't give her time to catch her breath. The hard swats landed one after the other, setting her bum ablaze as electric sparks raced up her spine and pooled low in her core. The endorphin rush meant she didn't know when he stopped until she was flat on the bed.

She didn't get time to see much of his room in the low light before his body pushed her into the mattress as he kissed her again. A deep and solid kiss. Harsh and ravenous, as if he had been starved of her for a decade.

She responded in kind, her legs wound around him while her arms pulled him even closer.

She had never been a wallflower. Never been the shy, retiring type when it came to their love affair. She had never been a passive participant.

She had always been there with him step by step, claiming him as he claimed her.

She had known from the first day he'd stood at the front of a class full of law students and introduced himself as Professor Bassong that she wanted him.

When the opportunity had arisen, she had grasped it and hadn't let go until things had gone horribly wrong. Now, she couldn't worry about the potential for things to go wrong again.

He covered her body with his large one, his hand cradling her head as his mouth took hers in rough and savage swipes.

She responded to his searing and demanding embrace, flesh and mind. Sparks raced down her skin. Her breasts grew heavy as her nipples hardened and ached.

"Oh," she moaned and rocked her hips as longing coiled in her belly, and the evidence soaked her shorts.

He tilted to one side as if in response to her need and stroked his hand down from her collarbone to mould her left breast.

Cotton fabric provided a barrier between their skins, but her body set ablaze. Her nipples stood in delightful torture as he grazed them.

He kissed and stroked her breast, and she became ready to combust. Prepared to burn to ashes.

How could it be that in all these years, she hadn't been able to stand the touch of another man? Yet, Zain could set her alight with a kiss, a stroke.

Intimate situations with her fiancé? She had always made excuses to avoid them. He had assumed she awaited their marriage before they got physical.

Something had to be wrong with her, she'd assumed at one time and had even gone as far as seeking counselling to resolve it.

Alas, nothing prevented her from becoming aroused, except her mind.

She needed the right man.

She needed Zain.

His lips travelled lower, and his teeth nipped her chin.

"Zain," she said in a husky voice.

He lifted his head. In the dim light, his expression acquired a hard, savage edge, his dark eyes piercing and consuming.

"Do you remember what it feels like to be mine? Let me remind you." He plundered her mouth with his tongue just as his hands worked to push her robe off her shoulders.

Their tongues tangled and tangoed.

Ten years apart, and nothing had changed.

Ten years apart, and everything had changed.

She didn't want finesse. She wasn't delicate.

She wanted Zain, raw and unrestrained.

She stroked her palms down his sides and tugged his T-shirt until she reached firm, hot skin.

He groaned and lifted his head, insatiable hunger blazing in his gaze.

"You need to remember what it feels like to be mine," she whispered to him, her voice hoarse.

The muscles on his back rippled as he leaned away, kneeling on the bed.

"I have always been yours alone." He spoke the vow in a deep, dark voice, as if he had reached into the depths of his soul and ripped the words out.

Their gazes locked, and time stretched to infinity.

Her breath caught. Could he have said what she thought he'd said? That there'd been no others since her?

Impossible. He might not be a king or president. But he proved to be a powerful and virile man.

No man could stay celibate for all those years.

Kweku had his mistresses. Their existence hadn't mattered.

But this?

Her heart clenched. She had spent all those years alone, aching for what she had lost. It seemed he had spent the time in the same way.

"And I have always been yours alone," she responded with equal passion. "There have been no others."

She had given her virginity to him. Afterwards, she couldn't bear another man's touch following the devastation she'd felt at his loss.

He sucked in a sharp breath as his eyes burned through hers.

"M'orae."

My precious one.

Her heart thudded against her chest. He hadn't used the affectionate expression since their break up. She'd thought she'd never hear the phrase again from him.

Tears pooled in her eyes, and she whispered the truth in return. "My beloved."

He returned to her, kissing her fiercely as he lifted her up. With callused hands on her skin, he tore her top over her head and yanked the shorts down her legs.

She tugged at his clothes, too, snatching raw kisses in between. A ripping sound filled the air. In her frenzy, she had split the fabric of his shirt. He sat on his hunches and tugged the rest of the tattered outfit off and then stood on the rug to push his shorts down.

He stood magnificent in the light pouring from the lounge through the crack in the door.

He proved to be everything she remembered and more. He had filled out with more defined muscles. His skin glowed like polished teakwood. Short hairs trailed down from his belly to the full erection jutting out proudly. And the beard on his face gave him a fierce aura. Her lover. Her dark warrior.

His blazing gaze held her in place as it roved her body, sending a heat wave over her skin. He soaked her in as much as she did the same.

She struggled to breathe as she lay naked and spread out on his bed.

He knelt on the mattress, his muscular thighs on either side of hers. His hand traced her face, in light feathery touches that made her tingle. He carried on in slow motion, working his way down to her collarbone and then to her breasts, which he teased and worshipped.

He lowered his head, and his mouth followed a similar path, renewing her passion in a blaze set by his touch.

When his fingers reached her trembling belly, his mouth covered her left nipple. He swirled his tongue around the taut flesh before he suckled it. Ache bloomed to pleasure.

She arched her body as his palm rested between her thighs.

He continued teasing her breast, occasionally adding the bite of his teeth, the coarse hair on his chin increasing the intensity.

Her breath came in short gasps, and there didn't seem to be enough air in the room, in the entire suite.

He changed over to the right breast, nipping and sucking as his palm cupped her mound. A finger caressed the edge of her slick opening but didn't delve in.

"Oh. Oh," she cried out and clasped his head with her hands. "Zain, stop teasing me."

He glanced up at her with a sexy wicked grin and his pink tongue rolling around her nipple. "What do you want?"

He licked the crevice between her breasts.

"I want you," she said in a breathless voice. Oxygen seemed in short supply and not getting to her brain. "I want everything you can give me. Right now."

"My demanding Ruby. I'm at your service." He gave her another wicked grin as he moved lower.

Surprisingly, his use of her middle name provided a level of intimacy that Isha didn't have. It meant he understood her like no others did.

He caressed her hips before spreading her thighs wide.

"Do you want me here?" His warm breath feathered her tender skin, his fingers spreading her labia.

"Yes," she muttered, fighting not to fall apart before he'd actually done anything.

He lowered his head between her thighs, then his tongue swiped from her slit upwards in a protracted, unhurried motion.

"Mmmmh." He groaned against her skin, sending micro shockwaves through her that contracted her inner channel in preparation for an orgasm.

"Oh," she moaned and canted her hips, wanting more pleasure.

His potent tongue worked her sensitive flesh, curling, sweeping, and flicking.

Her head dug into the soft pillows, and she gripped the sheets tight. Her breathing became desperate pants. Tension curled and twisted inside her.

His left hand returned to mould her breasts while the right teased her wet entrance.

She trembled, from deep inside, and tightened her grip on the sheets. Dizziness swept over her as she spun closer and closer out of control.

His tongue rolled around her clit as two fingers breached her slit. His bushy beard scratched her thighs.

"Oh," she cried out, arching off the bed.

His digits, more than two, thrust in and out just as he sucked the bundle of nerves.

"Zain!" She flew as her body quaked, higher and harder and faster.

She thrashed, and he held her, keeping her safe until she'd calmed.

He moved then, gliding his body back up until his substantial length prodded her entrance and his lips kissed hers.

He pulled her hand up and grasped her wrists, holding them as he stared down at her.

She gazed at him.

The muscles, the strength, the beauty of him.

The rugged face, sharpened by the cheekbones and beard. The brilliant black eyes that saw her need and matched it. The firm, sensual mouth that spoke to her soul.

Her heart lodged in her throat.

This was her man. Her Zain. Her beloved.

There would never be another man that held her heart the way he did.

"Say the words, M'orae." His voice sounded hoarse with emotion.

"My beloved," she replied with equal feeling.

Their fingers clasped together as he thrust into her, slowly and steadily. She ached at the intrusion. She hadn't welcomed his body in this manner for a long time. She needed to adjust to accommodate him. He didn't look away until he had sheathed himself fully inside her.

"I claim you with my heart and my body," he repeated the words he had spoken the first time they had made love, an ancient Ganuri vow that had bound his ancestors.

"And I claim you with my mind and my soul," she completed, binding them in a way they couldn't share with others.

Only then did he withdraw and ram back in, a force that travelled through her, snatching her breath and sending a wave of pleasure in return.

Hard and deep, he repeated the thrust, slow and measured, making her feel every sensation, every motion.

She rocked with him. Her desire rose with each movement, and she tightened her grip on his hands.

He lowered his head, kissing her. The bodies glided over each other as ripple after ripple of delight crashed through her. His pace quickened, and his grip tightened. He thrust harder and faster.

"Oooooh." She shattered into a million pieces, and fireworks exploded in her vision.

"M'orae," he cried out as he slammed into her again and again before going perfectly still.

CHAPTER TWENTY-ONE

ZAIN sat in bed, watching the woman asleep beside him.

Isha lay on her side facing him, her arm under the pillow where her head rested. The diamond earring on her right ear sparkled, catching the sunlight peeking through the edges of the heavy curtains covering the hotel windows.

The bed cover lay creased and tangled over their torsos. The delicious scents of their love-making perfumed the air.

His gaze travelled over her body, again and again, the tousled brunette hair feathering her beautiful face, her smooth, delicate neck, and the flawless bare shoulder and arm.

As always, he'd awoken at first light, and aside from a quick trip to the bathroom, he'd been unable to keep away from her.

A tingle spread across his chest, and his breathing became irregular.

Ruby—Isha lay in his bed.

The woman he'd thought he'd lost forever slept beside him.

Baring a quick stop to eat the cold dinner, they had made love for most of the night. A decade apart had made them insatiable.

He remained ravenous. His body swelled and hardened from watching her.

He could wake her by stripping the covers off, kissing and caressing every part of her before burying his dick inside her. She would welcome him in like she'd always done.

He wasn't a savage, though. No matter what some people thought of him.

Her body would be sore from frequent penetration. She needed to rest and recoup her energy, especially after the stress of the past week.

Occasionally, she would stir or sigh before settling, her breathing back in a soft-sounding pattern.

So he ignored his hunger for her and settled for watching her instead and accepting the joy of having her in his company.

Even if it would be for only a short time.

They couldn't stay in this hotel forever.

He had a nation to make, hopefully with her help.

And she had a wedding to attend, one that didn't involve him.

His chest squeezed tight, and the back of his throat hurt.

Last night, they had made vows unto each other. Perhaps they had spoken the words in the heat of the moment. Maybe to capture the bliss they had experienced with each other once.

In the light of day, did those words have any weight?

She remained the First Princess of Bagumi, a kingdom ruled by an absolute monarchy.

And he a man who believed in the democratic process, opposed to hereditary rulers. A man or woman should never rule a nation purely because of the accident of birth.

To wield absolute power over a country, one had to earn it and in some cases, fight for it. But it shouldn't be passed on based on bloodlines.

He had discussed his opinions about inherited kingdoms with Isha when they had first met, and they'd had heated debates about the pros and cons of absolute monarchies. They had even discussed the failed democracies of Africa.

All the time, he hadn't known she'd been a royal princess.

Now, he could understand some of the reasons she'd struggled to tell him the truth about her status.

A heart-wrenching sob filled the air.

He glanced at her face as he sat up and turned the lamp on.

Her eyes remained closed. She twisted to the right and the left, arms flailing.

"Isha," he spoke in a soft voice and placed a gentle hand on her shoulder.

A scream pierced the air, and she jerked upright, eyes wide, body trembling.

"Isha, you're safe." He kept his voice low and didn't reach for her in case he startled her.

She bent over, gasping for breath.

He massaged her bare back until some of the tension left her body.

She raised her head and looked at him. Her lovely brown eyes glimmered with tears.

"Hey, what happened?" He cocooned her with his body.

She snuggled into him and wrapped her arms around his neck, holding tight as if afraid to let go. She didn't say anything for about a minute.

He allowed her the time to get her bearings. The events of the past week must have unsettled her.

She leaned back and met his gaze.

"I dreamt that you left me pregnant and alone and heartbroken again. But this time, I was determined to find you, and I went to your house and found your mother mourning. You'd been killed."

Her eyes filled with tears.

"Hey, don't cry." He swiped the streaks with his thumb. "It was just a nightmare."

She gripped his arm. "No. It felt real. The heartache, the loss. It all felt real. Too real. I don't want to go through it."

"I'm sorry you had a nightmare about me. But I'm not going anywhere. I'm right here."

"I know." She covered her face with her palms. "Don't you get it? The dream was about your death. They are going to kill you because of MLG. You have to stop it. You have to give it up."

He took a deep breath and shook his head. Then, he got out of bed and pulled on the shorts he'd abandoned last night. He strode out into the living room.

"Zain, didn't you hear a word I said?" She scrambled off the bed, too, and grabbed what was left of her T-shirt.

"I heard you, Princess," he bit out and turned to face her, hand slashing the air. "So you want to tell me that after everything you've seen and everything you've heard in Ganuri, you want me to give up the fight for independence just because you had a dream."

"It is more than a dream. I have a bad feeling about this." She raised her hands in the air and let them flop. "Is Ganuri independence so important to you that you would risk your life for it?"

"Even before I started campaigning for independence, my life was risked several times over nothing. Isn't it better to die for something than to die for nothing, Isha? I know my purpose on this Earth. Do you know yours?"

"Uh," she growled in frustration. "You're so freaking obstinate. What about me? I've just reconnected with you. Do you think I want to watch you get killed?"

"What does it matter? In a few weeks, you'll be married to Doona."

Although she'd tossed her ring onto the dresser last night, Kweku Doona remained a shadow hovering over both of them.

She gasped, and her body froze. "What are you saying?"

"You tell me. You're the engaged one."

"Did you think that I would give my body to you and go back to him?"

"He's still the president's son, the future president, and I'm the leader of a rebel group, a pariah. I know which one your parents will approve."

She opened her mouth and closed it a few times, like a stunned fish.

"And I told you last night, I would have chosen you ten years ago. I choose you today. And I will choose you a thousand times."

"And give up being a royal princess? Your father will disown you."

She took steps towards him. "I doubt it will come to that. Whatever happens, I stand with you."

She stood close, staring up at him with sincere eyes.

He reached across and cupped her chin.

"Don't be fooled by this oasis of a hotel room. Life with me is arduous and dangerous. There will be no extravagance." He stroked his thumb over the jewel on her earlobe. "I cannot buy you diamonds."

Her lips curled up into a smile. "I have all the diamonds I want. Freeing the people of Ganuri is your purpose, and mine is to stand by you, come rain or shine. I made a vow to you last night, and you can be sure that I'm going to keep it."

He cupped her neck with both palms, stroking her mouth with his thumb. "You know the vows made in the privacy of heated passion are not valid if not backed up in public."

Her face furrowed in a frown. She jabbed her finger on his chest.

"If you're trying to break my heart, you are in for a surprise. I'm not budging. You couldn't move me even if you sent an armoured tank. You and I are joined, bound, tied together. Sooner or later, we are going to make that declaration in public. Is that clear enough for you, Professor Zain Bassong, or do I need to summon your security team to stand as witnesses?"

"I read you loud and clear, First Princess Isha Saene," he muttered as he dipped his head and covered her lips with his.

He kissed her deeply, his tongue tasting and savouring her mouth.

Softness and heat.

Sweetness and light.

She trembled and pressed against him, setting off an explosion in his veins.

Her tongue probed his mouth, and his tangled with hers. His nerve endings came to life, blood rushing to his groin, filling him until he throbbed with his need for her.

He nipped her lips, grazing their swollen tenderness.

She went pliant in his arms and moaned into his mouth.

He thrust his tongue into her, the way he hoped to piston his body into her warm, wet, welcoming one. He slid his hand into her tousled hair, massaging her scalp as he deepened the kiss.

Heat flushed his skin as he pressed his knees between her thighs, spreading them. She wore nothing under the long T-shirt.

His heart thumped hard, and blood whooshed in ears as her hands travelled up his chest, scorching his skin.

How could one woman have this much control over him? He'd never allowed another woman to get this close. He'd allowed Isha so many liberties and would give her so much more.

The kissing grew hotter, and he wanted more. His body tightened with desire.

He stroked his palm down her bare hip and between her legs. He met hot, wet, sensitive flesh.

Always so responsive, she gasped and jerked and shuddered as he caressed the bundle of nerves. He stroked her clit again, making her whimper and squirm. He sank his fingers inside her hot, damp core. Her channel muscles rippled around his digits, so tight and soft and warm. She rocked against him as if seeking more friction and more sensation.

"You're ready for me. I can't wait." The words came out strained.

"Don't wait." She reached down, dipped into his shorts, and grabbed his erection.

Wound so tight, he almost came. He gripped her hand and pressed his sweaty forehead to hers as he panted. "M'orae, don't."

"My beloved," she said in a sweet voice and batted her long lashes. "Will it help if I went on my knees and took you in my mouth?"

"No, it wouldn't." He growled and whirled her around, bending her over the arm of the sofa, her face down on the cushion.

Their relationship had always been physical and intense. They delighted in possessing each other, delighted in the irresistible chemistry between them.

He knelt behind her, stroked her from crack to cleft, finding slick, silky, and warm flesh.

Her smooth, round butt cheeks jutted out into the air, her labia and clit visible and pink against the flawless cinnamon skin.

The way the white top covered her upper body and left her lower half exposed, her body strewn over the arm of the settee, created an obscene image. Not a dignified posture for a princess.

She stared at him without fear or shame. Her longing remained open and palpable, her body trembling with her need as he caressed her.

She presented the most erotic picture he'd ever envisioned.

His Isha. His Precious One.

He stretched her thighs apart and settled between them. Dragging in a long breath, he leaned in and took the taut, aching clit into his mouth, sucking and licking.

"Holy ruler, Zain!" she cried out in a pleading voice.

He didn't relent, holding her legs apart as he jabbed and stroked.

She panted and squirmed, begged and groaned.

He teased and caressed with his tongue, prodded her clit before sucking and biting.

"Please. Oh, please, Zain." She shook, swinging her hips in desperation.

"Give me what I want first," he demanded as he jammed his finger inside her slick slit and drew her delicate tight bud into his mouth hard.

"Oh. Oh. Oh," she moaned as she climaxed in wave after wave, her body shuddering uncontrollably.

He didn't pull back, tasting her sweet surrender as she gushed onto his tongue.

He freed himself, discarding his shorts at his ankles as he rose. He didn't change her position before plunging deep into her warm, wet sheath. Another wave of orgasm slammed into her, rippling around his hard and tight cock.

He was ready to explode.

He'd been ready to explode from the moment she'd grabbed him earlier; a calculated move intended to turn him into an unrefined and primitive man driven by his baser urges. She had achieved the desired result.

It took sheer will power to hold off his impending release.

He gripped her hips and plunged into her again and again in deep, long thrusts. Pleasure skittered over his skin. He couldn't slow down, couldn't stop to think about anything else but the bliss rushing at him with the force of a tsunami.

He leaned over her, pressed his lips to the bare skin between her shoulder blades, just as he reached over and stroked her clit. "Fly with me."

She arched her back, jutted out her chest, hips grinding against his, and soared. Her quaking inner muscles triggered his release, and he sucked the skin on her shoulder as he came. They both trembled as he clung onto her for moments on end, their panting breaths harsh in the otherwise silent room.

Spent, he eased out of her and scooped her up and returned to the bedroom.

CHAPTER TWENTY-TWO

ISHA still floated on a post-coital cloud of bliss as she stepped out of the bathroom covered in the long white robe. She'd lost count of how many times she and Zain had made love since last night.

The last session had been a couple of hours ago. She'd had a nap before the breakfast he'd ordered arrived. They'd eaten before she'd come into her room for a shower.

She grabbed a short-sleeved sundress with a round neck from the wardrobe and laid it on the bed before using the coconut buttercream on her body.

Something on the dresser caught the light. A closer look showed it as her engagement ring.

Lips pressed together in a grimace, she turned away.

She had resolved all the old issues with Zain after their heated conversations last night and this morning.

Although she had removed Kweku's ring from her finger, the matter of her engagement to him was far from resolved.

Her family remained traditional when it came to many things, including marriage contracts.

Telling Kweku the wedding was off would be a lot easier compared to telling her parents that she loved Zain.

Whatever happened, she had pledged her heart and her life to the man she loved, and everyone else would have to get with the programme.

And the gaudy ring would be returned to Kweku.

Dressed, she stepped into the living area when a knock sounded.

"That must be the laundry service," Zain called out from the other bedroom. "Please give them the bags with dirty clothes."

"Sure," she replied and opened the door.

A girl in a blue check dress and white pinafore stood next to one of the security guards. "Good morning, madam. I came to collect the laundry."

"Morning," Isha replied. "The bags are over there."

The hotel staff walked over to the wall and picked the already filled linen bags. The bodyguard stood inside the room, holding the door as if he didn't want to leave the girl alone with Isha.

"How long before the clothes are ready?" Isha asked.

"A few hours. They should be done by this afternoon," Laundry Girl said.

"Good. Thank you."

"You're welcome."

The bodyguard closed the door when the girl left.

Isha found the remote control and switched the television on. She scrolled through to a news channel searching for any news about her abduction. Was it public knowledge? If her family didn't know her whereabouts, they would err on the side of caution and keep it private.

Zain came out of the bedroom. He had also showered and dressed in charcoal linen trousers and shirt.

Her breath caught. She forgot about her quest for news, enthralled by the smooth glide of his movements across the carpet.

"You are beautiful," he said before he kissed her, making her more breathless.

"You are the stunning one," she replied when they came up for air. "I'm simply dressed in a cotton dress."

"Whether the dress is cotton or silk, you look beautiful in it."

"I know. You told me." She smiled up at him and kissed his open mouth. "Glad to know I can still stun you."

"You always do." He took the remote control from her hand and switched off the TV.

"I was watching that," she protested.

"I have something better in mind." He pulled a phone out of his pocket. "I think you should call your family and tell them you're okay."

Jerking back, she stared at him incredulously. "You want me to call my parents? Are you serious?"

"I wouldn't say it if I wasn't. You've been missing for over a week, and if your parents are anything like mine, they would be worried about you. We sent them an anonymous message when you were taken that you were safe. But I know they won't rest until they hear or see you."

Her heart thumped hard against her chest, and dizziness swept over her. She lowered her body onto the sofa.

"I don't know what to say. Honestly, I'm worried about speaking to my parents. The minute I tell them where I am and how I got here, you'll be in trouble. There'll issue an international arrest warrant for you."

He sat on the sofa beside her. "I know. Of course, I don't want you to mention me or the details of how you got here. Not yet, at least. But it's up to you what you say to them."

She lowered her head onto her hands. She had been thinking last night about calling home and telling them her location so she could be picked up.

That had been before she had reconciled with Zain and had declared her feelings for him and vice versa.

Now, he offered her a gadget and his permission to contact home, after all.

This phone call would signal the end of their blissful moment together.

It would be time to face the real world outside.

For the first time in ten years, she lived again. Zain had renewed her zest for life. She wasn't ready to be separated from him. Not prepared to deal with her parents. However, her family would worry because of her disappearance. She needed to reassure them. Zain proved to be no danger to her.

Only one person would back her up one hundred per cent.

Her brother, Zik, was her champion and the keeper of her secrets.

She hoped he would keep another secret for her.

She lifted her head and looked at Zain. "I'm not going to call my parents. Not today, anyway."

His face puckered in a frown. "You're not?"

"No. I'll call Zik instead."

"Your older brother? The one I met."

"The same one."

"I suppose it makes sense since he already covered up for you in London."

"Exactly."

He puffed out a breath and held out the phone in her direction. "Okay."

She took the gadget, and he stood. She held his hand and tugged until he sat down beside her again.

"I won't mention my actual location, but is it okay to say that I'm in Ganuri?" she asked, wanting to avoid getting him in trouble.

"Sure," he replied, nodding.

"Also, I won't mention the MLG. Although I'd like to talk about you since he knows you already."

"Yes." He nodded again.

"Thank you." She pressed her lips to his briefly. "I'm going to be in the bedroom."

She walked into the room and shut the door, leaning on it for a few seconds. Then, she pressed the buttons to dial Zik's private line.

"Azikiwe Saene," he said in a deep, familiar voice after the second ring.

"Zik, it's me," she said.

"Isha, is that you?" He sounded breathless.

"Yes."

"How are you? Where are you? We've been worried sick."

"I'm fine. I'm sorry I went off the grid. I didn't mean to scare anyone."

"Are you sure you're okay? You disappeared from your party without telling anyone where you were going."

"I'm really sorry. I didn't mean to worry anyone. But everything got too much. I needed a break. Some space. I just had to get away for a little while."

"Well ... I can understand that, but you should have told somebody. Kojo didn't even know. He's out searching for you. We have teams searching for you. And there is no trace anywhere, although we haven't announced it publicly."

She wondered how the search team hadn't found her yet since she had been out and about in Ganuri. Then, she remembered there was a media blackout here, and there hadn't been any news crews at the locations she had visited.

"Call off the search for me. There's no need. I'm perfectly safe. I'll come home when I'm ready."

"You know I can't do that until I know where you are. You're a royal princess, the prime princess. You can't just wander off without others knowing your location."

"I don't want to be a princess for a few days. That's why I had to get away. Don't you ever feel like just being Zik without the titles or the protocols?"

"Sure, I do, sometimes. But I don't go running off into the wilderness."

She sighed. "I need this break, Zik. Please. Just let me have this time."

"Okay. Just tell me where you are and who you are with, and I'll call off the search party."

She scrubbed a hand over her face and walked over to sit on the bed.

"Wouldn't it be better if I don't tell you, so you have plausible deniability when Papa interrogates you?"

"We haven't told Papa that you are missing. You know he had a heart attack less than a year ago, and he already thinks the two of us are partners in crime. So when he finds out, he is going to accuse me of covering for you, anyway. So I'd rather know what's going on."

She sighed again. "It sounds fair. But before I tell you, promise me you won't tell anyone where I am or with whom."

"Isha—"

"Zik, promise me. Otherwise, I'm not telling you."

"Okay. Okay. I promise not to tell anyone your whereabouts or secret lover."

Her heart thudded. Secret lover? How did he know?

"What do you mean by a secret lover?"

"Come on, sis. The only other times you've behaved out of character or devised clandestine moves were when you were dating your lecturer in London. Now, you've disappeared for days and won't tell anyone what's going on. It has to be a man. Or a woman. But I don't think you swing that way."

Her cheeks heated. He knew her too well. "It is a man."

"I said it," he said enthusiastically and then calmed. "Is this about the wedding? Did you get cold feet?"

"This is more than cold feet. I'm with Zain."

"Zain?" He paused as if thinking. "As in Professor Zain Bassong?"

"Yes." She held her breath, wondering what he would say.

"Are you out of your bloody mind? After what he did to you?"

"Zik, calm down. It's not what you think. What happened back then was a big misunderstanding. We've talked, and we've reconciled. You know I love him. I've never stopped loving him."

"But you're engaged. Your wedding is only weeks away."

"Zik, listen to me. There isn't going to be a wedding."

"Isha, do you want to give your father a second heart attack? If so, you're on the right track."

A heaviness settled on her, and she didn't speak for several seconds as her mind warred with her heart. She didn't want to cause her family any distress. Perhaps Zik was correct, and she was out of her mind.

Zik puffed out a sober breath. "I'm sorry. I shouldn't have said that."

"No. You spoke the truth. I don't want to upset our parents. But I can't marry Kweku. I just can't."

"Okay. You know I'll support your decision. This road you're about to embark on won't be easy. Are you sure this Bassong guy won't abandon you like he did before?"

Who was ever one hundred per cent sure of anything?

Zain had made promises, and she believed he meant each of them.

"Zain is a good man. I trust him," she said.

"And I trust you. So I'll take your word for it. When are you planning to come home?"

"I don't know yet. But it shouldn't be long now. I want to ask you for another favour."

"Go ahead."

Isha swallowed. "Do you know anything about the situation in Ganuri?"

"Ganuri? The province with the rebels fighting to become a separate country from Wanai?"

"Yes. Can you speak to your friend is in military intelligence about sending a team out to the region to gather evidence?"

Zik chuckled. "Military Intelligence? Are you crazy? We can't send spies into Wanai. They are our allies. Can you imagine the diplomatic incident that will arise if Bagumi spies were discovered in Wanai for no good reason?"

"There are excellent reasons. The Wanain government is committing atrocities against its people. There is evidence of ethnic cleansing."

"Ethnic cleansing? Impossible."

"I've seen the evidence myself. The Ganuri people are systematically being wiped out. I've seen the graves, the burnt-out villages, the refugee camps. There's a media blackout and an economic blockade in the region. There is no Internet service, and mobile networks can only provide limited voice services."

"You're serious about this."

"I wouldn't joke about people's lives. We have to do something. If we can gather photographic evidence as well as eye-witness accounts, we can prevent more people from dying. Please do this for me. I won't ask you for another favour for a very long time."

"You'll owe me a big favour in return, and you know I'll collect."

"Name it, and it's yours."

"I'll hold you to that. So where exactly did all those things happen?"

She rattled out the locations she remembered. "We're going to need visual as well as audio recordings. Also, witnesses who can testify in a court of law will be great."

"You think it will get to that?"

"Someone needs to be accountable for all the deaths. They're not random occurrences. There will need to be an investigation at some point. For now, let's gather enough proof to warrant one."

"I'll speak to my friend and take it from there."

"Thank you so much. I'll call you again soon and find out how things are going."

"Good. Take care of yourself, and call me if you need anything."

"I will. My love to everyone. Tell them I'll see them soon."

"Will do."

"Love you, bro."

"Love you, sis."

Isha puffed out a relieved breath when she ended the call. Her shoulders lifted as if a weight had dropped from it.

CHAPTER TWENTY-THREE

A ringing sound woke Zain.

He sat up in bed, uncurled his body from Isha's as she stirred. The clock on the TV monitor read as one o'clock in the morning. He reached for the phone and dragged it to his ear.

"Prof, it's me. We've been compromised. We need to move immediately."

Samuel's urgent tone cut through his sleep haze.

"What happened?" he asked as his heart jolted.

"Can't explain now. Be ready to leave in five minutes."

"Okay." He put the phone back on the cradle without arguments.

Samuel was in charge of keeping him safe. And if the man said it was time to get out of the hotel, he wouldn't argue.

"Who was it?" Isha asked in a groggy voice.

"That was Sam. We have to go." His feet hit the carpet.

"Go where?" She sounded confused.

"We have to leave the hotel. Come on. Get up." He opened the drawer, grabbed underwear, tugged it on, and pulled a shirt over his head.

He glanced at Isha. She lay on her side, back asleep. He hurried across to her and hauled her out of bed.

"Isha, this is not a joke. It's not safe to stay here." He let her feet drop to the floor. "Put some clothes on, and pack your bags. We have to go in less than five minutes."

Her eyes went wide. "Oh. Okay."

She hurried across to the other bedroom where her clothes were located.

He pulled on a pair of jeans and shoved the rest of his clothes and belongings into the small suitcase. Feet in his boots, he glanced around the room and checked the en-suite, making sure he hadn't left any valuables behind.

He dragged the case to the door before going to check on Isha.

She wore a pair of jeans and a tank top, a pair of leather sandals on her feet.

"There's no time." He took the clothes she'd been trying to fold into the carry-on and squashed them in. Then, he cleared out the items on top of the dresser straight into the bag. "Check the bathroom."

She rushed in and came out with a small toiletries bag. "That's everything."

A knock sounded at the door, and then, Samuel called out from the living room, "Prof, we have to go."

"Did you let him in?" Isha sounded startled.

"He has a key in case of emergency. This is an emergency. Come on." He lifted her bag and walked out.

Samuel stood in the living room with two other bodyguards.

"Ready?" the man asked

"Yes." Zain put Isha's suitcase next to his.

"Don't worry if you've left anything. My men will clean the place and wipe out fingerprints. Anything valuable will be reunited with you later. I have a guy in the control room to make sure there is no CCTV recording your departure, the same way we deleted your arrival."

One of the bodyguards carried the two suitcases and headed out.

Zain took Isha's hand and led her out of the room while Samuel followed behind.

Ten minutes later, they were in the car and on the road in a two-car convoy. The third car was for the guys cleaning the hotel suite who would join them later.

Their headlights showed only the black SUV in front. This early in the dark morning, there were no other cars on the road.

"Samuel, tell me what's going on," Zain demanded in the silence of the car.

Samuel twisted in his seat, looked at Isha, and then at Zain with his brow raised.

"Whatever it is, you can say in front of Isha," he added, knowing that whatever had caused them to flee the hotel in the middle of the night was probably for MLG ears only.

But Isha was part of him, which made her part of MLG.

He wouldn't hide anything from her.

"I've ordered Latifah to take Mama away from Boma. Doona issued a warrant for your arrest," Samuel said without blinking.

Isha gasped. "What? Why?"

"Why don't you tell us?" Samuel said in a harsh voice.

"Watch your tone," Zain bit out.

"What is he talking about?" Isha asked, concerned.

"Don't worry about it," he tried to soothe her.

"He thinks it's my fault, doesn't he?" She reached across and grabbed his hand. "You don't think I had anything to do with it, do you? I didn't tell Zik what really happened. I just told him I was visiting you."

"Maybe he told Kweku where you were."

"He wouldn't. He promised he wouldn't. You believe me, don't you?"

"I do."

But at the back of his mind, doubt niggled. Was it merely a coincidence that the day he'd allowed her to call her family was the day a warrant had been issued for his arrest?

* * *

Isha and Zain sat on a boat going up the river. The early morning fog made the sky and water and dense foliage blend together in a blue-green-grey mist. The scenery disappeared and appeared, moving and altering, like a ghoul or a changeling.

They had travelled all night from the hotel. First in the car to the point where the vehicle couldn't go any further, and then on foot across the hills, and now on boats.

They hadn't spoken much since their conversation in the car when Samuel had practically accused her of betraying Zain.

Although she had denied it, she couldn't be altogether sure that he believed her.

Just when she'd thought they'd reached a reasonably stable point in their relationship, something else had come along to knock them off course.

She had to believe that her brother hadn't told anyone, least of all Kweku, about their conversation. If she couldn't trust her brother, then she'd landed in hot water.

Who else would have revealed their situation?

The only other people who knew about her were Zain's security team and his domestic staff at home.

Why would they wait until now to reveal her presence? It made no sense.

She'd hate to think that one of his own would be this treacherous.

They travelled another hour or so before getting off the boats and stomping through marshy terrain, then up an incline. Ahead, a wooden structure appeared out of the mist. It looked like a small hut at first. As they walked closer and the fog cleared, she realised it wasn't just one but a cluster of wooden cabins on stilts designed to blend into the environment.

The men carrying the supplies went ahead of them into one of the huts. When they came out, Zain took her hand and climbed the short steps.

The interior was split into two spaces, the first one almost empty with a small table and wooden chair while the other had a cot barely large enough for two people.

"We're going to have to stay here for a few days," he said, sounding tired for the first time since they'd left the hotel.

"Okay." She glanced around and tried to tease him to lighten the mood. "It's not exactly The Ritz."

He met her gaze, but there was no humour. "I know this is not what you're used to—"

"Shhh." She pressed her finger to his downturned lips. "You warned me that life with you would not be easy. I came here willingly, remember?"

"You deserve better than this."

"It will be just for a few days, and everything will be cleared up."

***

Isha lay on the cot beside Zain, the kerosene lantern on the floor flickering.

The hut didn't have electricity, and the generator only stayed on for an hour a day to charge small electronic devices. There were no mod cons. The food was cooked and eaten on the day. She had to go to the stream meandering through the forest to wash her body and clothes. The drinking water was boiled and filtered.

A few days had turned into two weeks at the safe house.

Zain kept his outward composure towards her. Signs showed more went on in his mind. He became quiet, moody even, a man she didn't recognise. He wasn't designed to go into hiding. He faced his challenges regardless of how much he suffered.

Thankfully, his mother was in hiding too, far from the clutches of the Wanai Secret Police who had returned to his house in Boma.

The weight of the troubles of his people and the days in isolation lay heavy on his shoulders, making him fragile with exhaustion, breaking him into pieces.

She'd heard him arguing with Samuel about her. Tired of talking and negotiating with little results, Samuel wanted the men armed and facing off with Doona.

Now, he turned his head and glanced at her.

Her heart cracked at the lack of a smile. The blissful day they'd spent in the hotel now seemed ages ago.

Dark circles outlined his eyes, and his onyx irises had lost their sparkle.

He remained insanely gorgeous.

Her heart raced as they lay in the dim room without saying a word.

She traced her fingers along the welts zigzagging his back. Old wounds, they looked as if they had been systematically inflicted.

She'd asked him about them before, and he'd dismissed her. He hid something important from her.

"Zain, please tell me how you got these scars. You didn't have them when I first met you years ago," she said in a low voice.

Although he lay on his stomach and hadn't spoken for minutes, he remained awake. His breathing hadn't evened out like it did when he slept.

"Isha, do not worry about the scars," he murmured.

He rolled over, shifted up the bed, so his head leaned on the make-shift bamboo headboard. More lines had appeared around his eyes, and his skin was drawn.

She didn't look that much better, either. She'd dropped a dress size since her arrival in Ganuri, and without the usual modern amenities in their hideout, she would hardly win the Princess of the Year Award.

None of that mattered.

Her concern about his mental state heightened.

He wasn't a man built for isolation. He thrived when he engaged with people, whether in a classroom or courtroom or protest rally.

This forced seclusion was killing him, his mind and soul.

Watching him was like watching a windscreen crack under the weight of a boulder—one smash in the middle creating rivers of breaks that rippled outwards until the whole thing crumbled into shards.

"You can talk to me."

"I am."

"You're not," she scolded. "Something happened to you when you left London. You can't let it fester inside you."

"I've never spoken about those scars to anyone. What good will it do to talk about them now?"

She moved her head side to side in a slow, disbelieving manner.

Anger boiled inside her beneath the hurt that gripped her throat. She swallowed.

"Do you think it was easy for me to tell you about losing our baby? It is a part of my life I wanted to bury. Talking about it made me re-live the distress and anguish. And in the end, it freed me because I'm no longer carrying the burden alone. We cannot let anything come between us again, especially not our pasts." She challenged him.

In the dim orange lamplight, his gaze became unreadable.

"No matter what they did to you, you're still the most stunning man I know. You're strong and full of empathy. Nothing is going to change the way I feel about you. Nothing."

He sat up and ran a hand over his face. "I'm keeping this part of me away from you because it's not nice. It's dark and ugly, and in the light of day, you won't like it."

"I need you to tell me." She gripped his hand, her voice barely above a whisper.

They stood in a storm, and she needed to know the man inside out as much as he knew her inside out.

Her spine prickled with awareness. "Zain, please—"

"Okay," he said in a choked voice as he lifted their entangled fingers to his lips. "I was never able to hide from you ten years ago. Be warned. I'm not the same man you met in London."

His lids fluttered shut, and his thick lashes formed crescent shadows on his cheekbones. But she didn't miss the watery shimmer they locked away.

Her heart wrenched, and she fought the burning ache in her throat. She pulled their joined hands to her lips and kissed the back of his feverishly and reverently, wanting to reassure and soothe with equal measure.

He lifted his lids and met her gaze. The awareness returned to her spine at the openness displayed in the depths of his onyx eyes. He bared his soul to her through his eyes. Their hearts beat in sync, and they were one. Soul mates.

She nodded in understanding and pressed their joined hands to her lips again.

She traced her fingertip across round dark marks on his chest not more substantial than five pennies in diameter. "What are these?"

He didn't even look down at where she touched as he held her gaze. The orange flame flickered in his eyes as his lips tightened.

"Those are cigarette burns."

"Cigarette burns? How? You don't smoke." Then, the penny dropped. "Someone burnt you on purpose. When did that happen?"

There were too many scars for them to be accidental.

How dare anyone do this to him?

"When I was arrested for the first time by the WSP, it was part of their torture regime. They did other things, as well."

"Who did this to you?" Her anger flared. Someone was going to pay for this, or the Wanai Secret Police would face her wrath.

"It doesn't matter now." He lifted her hand and placed a kiss on her fingertips.

She tugged her arm back. She would not let this go.

First, the WSP had nearly killed his mother, and then, they'd tortured him. Enough was enough.

"Of course, it matters. Tell me the freaking SOB that tortured you, damn it."

He scrubbed his hands over his face and let out a sigh. "The same man who threw Mama off the balcony burnt his cigarettes on my chest."

"Huh? Kweku did this?" Isha froze. Her mind reeled. "Kweku tortured you?"

What the freaking Hell? What kind of a man had she been engaged to? How had she not seen him for the devious person he was?

She scrambled off the bed and paced. The place was cramped. She barely took five steps before she had to go the other way.

Images and conversations bombarded her as something niggled in her mind.

"Why did they arrest you?" She paused to stare at him.

"Trumped-up charges. They claimed they were investigating my alleged links to an illegal organisation, which was ridiculous because MLG was not even formed then. I was a university lecturer, for goodness' sake. He threw my mother off a balcony, knowing that would make me come home, and he arrested me at the airport. I was locked in isolation for days and tortured while my mother was in the hospital fighting for her life."

Oh, no! Her stomach heaved, and nausea rose. She swivelled, ran through the hut, and yanked open the exterior door.

Samuel and another man standing outside turned in her direction. She charged out towards the trees, leaned forward, and threw up.

"What's going on?" someone asked.

"Get me some water," Zain said before his palm settled on her back.

She stayed bent over as she tried to catch her breath and quell her stomach.

Footsteps thudded on the uneven planks forming a gangway. Zain pushed a toothbrush and metal cup of water towards her. "Clean your mouth."

She rinsed her mouth with the water before brushing and spitting out the paste. Zain gave her a towel to wipe her mouth. Then, he led her to a fallen tree trunk they used as a bench near the open fire. The damp night air made the flames crackle.

"Are you okay?" he asked, watching her as if she were a fragile egg.

"I'm okay. I just want to clarify something. When you left London ten years ago and told me you were going home because of a family emergency, it was because your mother had fallen from the balcony?"

"Yes. I didn't know what had actually happened. I got a message that my mother was in the hospital, and I should come home immediately."

She nodded and swallowed the bile in her throat. "And when I couldn't reach you for days after that, it was because you had been arrested."

"Yes. I spent five days in WSP custody."

She swallowed again as her stomach knotted. She dreaded asking the question. But it had to be asked. She had to know for sure.

"About two weeks after you left London, I got an email from you telling me our relationship was over. Did you send that email?"

He reached across and took both her hands in his, his head bowed. "Yes, I did."

"It was because of Kweku, wasn't it?" she gritted out.

His head rose sharply, and he looked at her with a brow raised. "How did you know?"

"It all slotted into place as soon as you told me that he arrested you ten years ago. He was the one who told you I was a princess, wasn't he?"

"Yes, he was." Zain's eyes narrowed. "He showed me photos of the two of you and claimed you'd been dating while you were also with me. He tortured me and threatened to kill my mother if I ever contacted you again."

"Oh, I'm going to kill him. I'm going to freaking kill him." Anger boiled inside, spilling out in her words. She balled her hands and shook her head.

How could she have trusted such a swine?

"He said your father had given him permission to deal with me."

"That's not true. My father would never be a party to torture."

"How can you be so sure? The week I got arrested, his father was on a state visit to Bagumi, and it seems your families are close."

She frowned. "No. I can't believe my father would condone his actions. Kweku became a friend of the family through Zawadi. They met at the military academy and grew close. He's been a welcome family friend for about fifteen years. I just never thought him capable of the devious things he has done. I was freaking engaged to the sonofabitch."

Her world tilted. She played back memories of them together all those years ago. How had Kweku found out about her relationship with her professor?

She groaned as she pictured all the horrors that Zain had suffered because of her. Imagined his anguish at knowing his mother was broken in a hospital ward while he'd been locked up, incapable of helping her.

In light of everything, she didn't deserve him. Didn't deserve his love.

How could she ever make it up?

"That's all in the past," Zain said in resignation.

"No, it's not. He's still doing the same things. He violated your civil liberties. He nearly killed Mama. He abused his position as the son of the president. He should be brought to justice."

"Justice? Look around you, Isha. Justice in Wanai is as corrupt as the murky waters at the bottom of the river. There can never be justice for as long as Doona or any member of his family is in charge of this country."

"Then it's time to unseat the Doonas from power."

Everything went quiet. Even Samuel and the other guard who had moved to the far side of the campfire fell silent, making it apparent they had been eavesdropping.

"What are you saying?" Zain asked in alarm. "Unseating Doona might involve going to war, and the last time I checked, you were a pacifist."

"It's easy to be a pacifist when you're living in the lap of luxury, and your home isn't being invaded, or your children being raped and murdered." She turned to address the men in the far corner, rising to her feet and raising her voice. "Is this what you signed up for? To hide out here while a tyrant destroys your country?"

"Of course not," Samuel retorted. "We're here because of you. He wants to protect you."

"Zain?" She looked down at him. "Is this true? Are we here because of me?"

He straightened and clasped her shoulder. "I saw the fear in your eyes when you woke up from the nightmare about my death. I can't protect you if I'm locked up in Doona's prison."

She cupped her palm against his cheek. "Yes, I was afraid after that nightmare. But I'm even more afraid of seeing you like this. This isolation is destroying you. More to the point, it is not helping the people of Ganuri. You were not meant for the shadows. You were meant to stand in the light."

"Standing in the light gives Doona a visible target to shoot," he said in an amused tone.

"That's where Samuel and co get to shine." She raised her voice so the other man would hear. "It is his job to make sure Doona misses his target."

Zain smiled, the first time for days. "You are serious about this."

"Absolutely. You are a symbol of hope for the people of Ganuri. We need to keep your light burning bright and out in the open."

CHAPTER TWENTY-FOUR

THE next day, they packed up and returned to the city. The journey downriver in the boats and the hike across the forest to the safe house where they'd left the cars didn't seem as gruelling in the daylight as it had been when they'd done it at night.

She managed to catch a nap during the four-hour drive back to Boma.

When they arrived at Zain's house, she left the men to debrief while she had a hot shower, the first one since their stay in the hotel two weeks ago.

It felt great to have pinpricks of hot water on her skin in an enclosed sparkling glass cubicle compared to the cold water that had come from a make-shift shower installed in an outside shack at the forest cabin.

There might be no gold taps or marble bidets in this house. Still, this was luxury.

She stayed under the sprinkle for longer than usual but got out reluctantly in a bid to save water. She'd just finished getting dressed when a knock sounded on the bedroom door.

"Come," she said, thinking it was probably Zain checking in on her.

The door pushed in, and her bodyguard stood there behind Zain.

"Kojo!" she screamed as the man stepped in. She rushed over and hugged him tightly. "It's so good to see you."

"It is, My Princess. How are you?" He stepped back to look her over.

"I'm doing fantastically well and even better with seeing you." She turned to Zain. "Thank you so much for letting him come here."

Zain shoved his hands in his pockets. "I had little choice in the matter. I'll leave you two to catch up."

He shut the door as he left.

"Your Highness, are you really okay?" Kojo asked as soon as they were alone, his voice laced with suspicion.

She tilted her head. "Of course, I'm doing great. I know you must have been worried when I disappeared. But don't be. Zain has taken care of me."

"Taken care of you? He abducted you, My Princess."

"He may have taken me without my consent, but I'm here now because I want to be."

"Really? So you can leave?"

"Yes, I can. But I don't want to."

"But what about your family? The king?"

"I spoke to Zik two weeks ago, which reminds me, I need to call him soon. What about you? How did you get here? Did Zik tell you where I was?"

"No. After you disappeared, I spoke to Zawadi and Kweku. I knew I couldn't go back to Bagumi without finding you, or it would be my neck for the guillotine. So I searched for you, following several dead-end leads until I came across Latifah."

"You met her? She is Zain's second-in-command. I haven't met her yet."

"You've met her. She was the one who sedated you at the party."

"That was Latifah?" She recalled the cold eyes of the woman who had injected her and shuddered.

"Yes, that's her. She is tiny and deadly."

She looked up at him with a smile. "You sound as if you had a very close encounter with her."

He shifted and averted his gaze. She could have sworn that he blushed.

He cleared his throat. "It's a long story, My Princess. The short of it is that I found her, and she brought me to Ganuri three weeks ago. We were told that you had gone on a trip with the professor. Then two weeks ago, we had to take Mrs. Bassong and Aliyah to Burkina Faso to stay with a friend. I'm just pleased to find you well now."

"I'm so glad that you are well, too, my dear Kojo."
***

Isha sat with Zain in his private quarters. They had finished dinner and lay curled up on the settee.

The day had been filled with activities, Zain's meeting with his team, and then visitors coming and going. He'd recorded a speech addressed to the people of Ganuri that was scheduled for broadcast. She had called Zik who'd said he waited to hear back from the team sent to document the atrocities in Ganuri.

This was the first chance they'd had to be alone.

He placed the newspaper he'd been reading on the side table. "We need to talk."

"This sounds ominous," she said as she shifted to face him.

"I have information that Doona is coming here tomorrow to arrest me. He knows you are here."

"He does? How come?"

"I told my team to spread the information so that his spy will pass it on."

"Oh. So what happens now?"

"You may not know my team very well. They are all good people trying to do the best they can. Samuel and Solomon come across as brutes, but they wear their hearts on their sleeves. Once they get to know you, they are the most loyal people you will come across. They will fight for you and die for you. Latifah is the hard nut to crack. She won't show you her intentions until the very last moment. All you have to pray is that you're not on the receiving end of her lethal actions."

"Yes, she is scary."

He smiled. "She will protect you. If anything happens to me, go with what she says. She's the one most likely to have a clear head. Sam and Sol get too emotional."

"Okay. But nothing is going to happen to you."

"That's the hope. But it's good to be prepared regardless."

She reached out and took his hand. "I'm prepared. You shouldn't worry, either. You won't be in jail for very long and not at all if I can help it. He has no grounds to arrest you."

"Kweku can be heavy-handed. I don't want you to provoke him."

"I'll be just fine." She patted his hand and leaned in to brush her lips against his. "He wouldn't dare to harm me. I am the First Princess of the Kingdom of Bagumi and an outstanding lawyer, too."

He grinned and returned her kiss, which turned passionate in moments.

That night, they made love in slow, measured movements as if recording each other for posterity. They spoke words of love and held one another even after the embers had quenched and they were sated.

Before dawn, they woke, made love in the shower as they cleaned each other, and later dressed in near silence.

Breakfast was also early. Isha pushed the food around on the plate, her stomach in knots and unable to take much in. Zain had to eat. They weren't sure when next he would get a decent meal.

Afterwards, they sat in the living room and waited with Latifah, Samuel, Solomon, and Kojo.

The atmosphere felt as if Zain was a man on death row awaiting execution.

The sound of sirens filled the air.

"They are here." Samuel got up and went to the door.

The knot in Isha's belly tightened. Chills travelled down her spine as her skin got clammy.

It was happening.

Zain reached for her trembling hand and squeezed.

She glanced at his face.

He appeared dignified and composed, a mix of the academic and the lawyer. None of his turmoil showed.

How could he be so calm? Rattled, she almost fell apart, and Kweku wasn't even in here yet.

She swallowed her apprehension and focused on keeping a composed appearance.

There was a banging sound outside, followed by shouting. Then footsteps stomped through the entryway.

Kweku appeared at the entrance in full military regalia, followed by other men in uniform.

"Gentlemen, do come in," Zain said and didn't get up from his seat on the sofa.

Kweku ignored his remark, his gaze focused on Isha. "Princess, it is a surprise to see you here."

"Is it?" she replied in a haughty tone. "I came to visit a friend. What are you doing here?"

"Visit a friend?" He frowned.

"Didn't I tell you? Zain is an old friend of mine. I'm spending some time with him, catching up on old times."

Kweku's jaw tightened. "We have information that Mr. Bassong and his terrorist group kidnapped you from Lagos about a month ago. I am here to arrest him and take him in for questioning."

Isha let out a stilted laugh. "Kidnapped? Do I look like I have been kidnapped? No chains are holding me here."

She lifted her arms to prove her point.

"In which case, you can come with me," he bit out.

"No. I told you I'm visiting Zain. I'm not ready to leave."

Kweku looked ready to explode, his face puffing up. "I order you to leave this house immediately."

Zain's grip tightened on her hand. "Don't—"

"Hang on a minute," she cut him off. "Did you order me to leave this house? Who died and made you king?"

"I'm the head of the WSP and your fiancé. You do whatever I say."

She jerked upright. "I am the First Princess of the Kingdom of Bagumi, and you are out of order."

His hands balled into fists, and he rolled his neck, jaw tight. "In which case, you are an illegal alien in Wanai, and I will place you under arrest."

Isha's head swam, and her stomach dropped. "You're going to arrest me?"

"Yes." He gritted out. "Unless you come with me willingly."

Holy ruler, what now? How was she going to get out of this without dropping Zain in it?

"You can't arrest her. Of course, she has a valid visa to be in Wanai," Zain responded before she could say anything.

He squeezed her hand as he glanced at her. "Your passport should be in your bag upstairs. Perhaps your assistant can get it for you."

She hadn't seen a passport since her arrival. Did Kojo bring hers when he came to Boma?

"Of course. Kojo, please be kind and fetch my passport for me," she said, glad her voice hadn't betrayed her unease.

"If you will allow me, Your Highness. I will get the passport," Latifah said in a demure voice and headed upstairs, followed by Kojo.

Tense silence hovered in the room as they waited for Latifah's return.

Isha's heart thumped hard against her chest, and sweat trickled down her spine.

She couldn't remember being in a more high-strung situation.

She didn't know if there was a passport or whose passport they would try to pass off as hers. Kweku had seen her passport previously, so should be able to detect a fake document.

On the upside, she had acquired a visa to visit Wanai a few weeks before her abduction. So she had a valid entitlement. It just needed to be stamped by Wanai Immigration Service.

"Can I offer you a drink?" Zain asked as if he entertained a guest.

"I don't want a drink," Kweku snapped and pointed at Zain. "You can sit there and look smug, but I will deal with you shortly."

That pissed Isha off, and she forgot about the passport situation. "I will advise you not to threaten my client, Mr. Doona."

"Your client?"

"Yes, I'm a lawyer, and it seems Mr. Bassong requires legal representation since you seem intent on arresting him. So I am offering my services." She glanced at Zain.

He winked at her.

She puffed out a breath and held the next one as Latifah returned.

"Here is the passport, sir," Latifah said.

"And who are you?" Kweku snatched the object and scrutinised the pages.

"I am First Princess Isha Saene's assistant," she replied. "Do you need my passport as well, sir?"

He eyed her, shook his head, and returned to check the document in his hand.

Isha's heart raced. From where she sat, the passport looked genuine enough, but she couldn't tell.

"I want to talk to Ms. Saene privately," Kweku said.

Isha's heart jolted.

"Is there a problem with the passport?" Zain stiffened.

"That's yet to be determined. I just need to question the princess privately." Kweku closed the document.

Zain nodded at the others but didn't move from his chair. Everyone stepped out of the living room.

"You will have to excuse us, too, Mr. Bassong." Kweku glared.

"I'm not leaving her alone with you." Zain placed the ankle of his right leg on his left knee, his right hand on his thigh and left hand clasped with Isha's.

"Whatever you want to say to me, you can say in front of Zain," she said.

"If that's the way you want to play it." Kweku lowered his body into an armchair. "Have you forgotten that you are my fiancée, and we are getting married soon?"

"Your fiancée? That's laughable, isn't it? You were threatening to arrest me a short while ago. And somehow, you think I'm going to marry you?"

"What am I supposed to do? You disappear for weeks, and when I find you, you refuse to come with me." He tossed the passport at her.

She shook her head.

"You're unbelievable. Any reasonable human being will take the hint and realise that he's been dumped. Instead, you turn up here and throw threats around like mini grenades." She shifted forward and shoved her hand into the pocket of her sundress. "Let me be absolutely clear in case it hasn't been clear enough. I am not going to marry you. Our relationship is over. You can have your ring back."

She tossed the jewelled hoop at him.

He caught it and stared at her incredulously. "You are breaking off our engagement."

"That is correct." She sat primly, projecting haughty princess.

"It's because of him." He glared at Zain.

"Partly correct. But mostly because you're a sonofabitch."

"How dare you?" He shot off the chair, eyes blazing, and stomped towards her.

In a flash, Zain stood in front of her, intercepting him. His hands balled into fists by his sides.

"I told you to never get in touch with her again," Kweku shouted. "I told you what would happen if you did."

"No. Your mother!" Isha stood and clutched Zain's arm, her heart racing. "He's going to kill her."

"He's bluffing," Zain said, body tensed.

"Am I? I know she's in Burkina Faso. All it will take is a phone call, and boom." He jerked his hands apart like an explosion.

"Sonofabitch." Zain leapt forward, hands raised to choke Kweku, who jumped back.

"Zain, no." She held him back. "Don't give him a reason to arrest you."

"Yes, Zain. Do what the little woman wants," Kweku mocked.

Zain jabbed his right hand, and the punch landed on Kweku's chin and sent him careening into the armchair.

Isha's breath hitched, and she covered her mouth with her palm as Zain shook out his hand.

Kweku pulled a handgun from his hip strap and pointed it at Zain's head. "You're going to pay for this. Raise your hands, Zain Bassong. You're under arrest."

CHAPTER TWENTY-FIVE

"NO!" Isha scrambled to stand in front of Zain. "Please, he didn't mean to hit you."

"Isha, it's okay," Zain said and placed his hands on her shoulder.

"No." She glanced at him as the fear of the nightmare returned. She had the feeling if Zain went with Kweku now, he would never return. "Kweku, listen to me. I'll go with you instead if you leave Zain and his mother alone."

"Isha, no." Zain sounded adamant.

She swivelled to face him and raised her hand to cup his cheek.

"I know what he's capable of doing to you. I saw those scars on your body and Mama's injury. I can't let him do that to both of you again." Her eyes clouded over, and she swallowed down the hurt at the back of her throat. "He can't hurt me. I'm still a member of a royal family."

"You don't need to do this." He gripped her arms.

"I do. Please understand." Her heartbeat raced, and her throat became sore as desperation gripped her. She would do anything to prevent Kweku from hurting him again.

He dropped his hands, and his face hardened. "If that's what you want."

Her heart crumpled because she would break a promise she'd made to him. But she couldn't let Kweku take him. Not again.

She turned back to Kweku. "If I go with you, then you promise to leave the Bassong family alone forever. No more abuse disguised as arrests. No more assaults camouflaged as accidents. Do we have a deal?"

He sheathed his weapon and twisted his lips in a smug smile. "If you agree to make no contact with the Bassongs in future, and marry me, then we have a deal."

"Deal," she said. "Give me a few minutes to pack my things."

"Wait." He pulled out the ring from his pocket. "You have to wear this."

He dropped the engagement ring into her palm. "Put it on."

"Not yet. I'll wear it when I leave."

Her stomach rolled at the thought of wearing the symbol. She'd already hurt Zain enough by agreeing to go with Kweku. She wouldn't wear the ring and rub it in his face.

She picked up the passport and grabbed Zain's hand. "Please come with me."

She needed to talk to him without others overhearing.

Zain didn't budge.

She tugged again. "Please."

With a glare in Kweku's direction, he relented, following her out of the room and up the stairs.

"Kojo, please make sure my things are ready to go," she said as she walked past her bodyguard.

"Yes, Your Highness," he replied.

Zain pulled her into his room, shut the door, pushed her against it, and gripped her hands above her head.

"You're mine," he growled before he crushed her mouth with his in a brutal, punishing kiss that would surely leave her mouth swollen and bruised.

"I'm yours," she replied, between caresses, her throat clogged up.

Her pulse rate skyrocketed, and a tremor passed through her as his rigid body braced hers against the wall. His knee parted her thighs. Heat sizzled down her skin, and her breaths came in shallow pants as he kissed her cheek and neck.

"Isha, you said you wouldn't go to him," he ground out, sounding hurt as he released her hands.

"I did. I'm sorry." She must seem unreliable and untrustworthy after everything.

She gripped his head with both hands and tried to make him look her in the eyes so he would know she spoke the truth. "I'm only going for a little while to buy you some time. My brother will come through for us with those videos. I know he will. And then, we'll have some leverage."

Bundling up the hem of her dress, he cupped the junction of her thighs, making her hot and squirmy.

"I don't like it. I hate the thought of him being alone with you." He pressed his forehead to hers. "Latifah will go with you as your assistant. That's the only way I'll be at peace."

"Okay," she breathed out in acceptance.

"Promise me he won't touch you." He ran a hand up the inside of her thigh.

She arched and inhaled and pulled him against her. The heat of his erection rubbed her belly. She hooked her leg over his hip and leaned in to kiss him, but he jerked back.

"Promise me, damn it." He pressed his palm around her neck, holding her in place.

His hand ran inside her leg and reached the elastic band of her panty.

"I promise I won't let him touch me." Overtaken by a primal need, she felt wild and hot, and she wanted him. She didn't know when next she would see him.

She clung to his shoulders and hooked her right leg to his hip so that she straddled him.

Beyond the door, everyone waited for them, for her to go with Kweku. Right now, she didn't care about anyone else but the man she clung on to.

She wanted him. She had always been his, ten years ago, today, and forever.

He slid a finger beneath the fabric of her knickers and stroked her moist heat. She jerked and shuddered as he teased and stroked her clit while he kissed her shoulder and collarbone.

She whimpered and writhed. "Remind me what it feels like to be claimed by you."

A zipping sound filled the air, and then, he plunged his rigid erection inside her.

"Oh," she cried out, her body arching in pain and pleasure.

Hard and snug, he stroked inside her, and her muscles rippled around him.

He drew out and thrust in, the pace urgent and wild and impatient. She bucked against him and whimpered, possessing him just as he owned her. Filled with longing, hunger. Need. She got lost in the sensation of him and them together.

Just as she cried out, he covered her mouth with his and came inside her.

CHAPTER TWENTY-SIX

THE trip from Boma to the Wanai Presidential Palace took about two hours. First, the drive to the airport, then a private jet to the capital city, and then the short tour to the residence.

Isha didn't say much to Kweku throughout the trip. When she did reply to his questions, it was with one-word answers.

She didn't want or need to speak to him.

All she had to do was bid her time until she got confirmation from Zik about the investigative team in Ganuri. Once they had the proof needed, she would be back with Zain.

As soon as they arrived, the place bustled with staff running around and attending to them. She retired to the quarters assigned to her, which was an apartment with rooms for Latifah and Kojo.

Kojo did a sweep of the suite to make sure there were no recording devices installed within the walls. None were found.

The rest of the day she spent on phone calls, first to her family, then to Amnesty International and the International Criminal Court that prosecuted individuals for political crimes like genocides, war crimes, and crimes against humanity.

The feedback was the same as she already knew. She needed visual evidence and eyewitnesses if possible.

Zik confirmed he would hear back from the covert team the next day. Then, she could file a formal case with the ICC.

That night, sleep proved elusive.

She was surrounded by luxury and on a bed covered with expensive sheets. The air-conditioner kept the room at a moderate temperature, and she had household staff on her beck and call.

Yet, she would swap it all for the little bamboo cot in the humid wooden cabin in the middle of the forest where she had to wash her clothes at a stream as long as she could be with Zain.

Still, she had to do this, had to make this deal with the devil to keep Zain and his mother safe.

She wondered what he was doing and how he was coping.

Would it be possible to get a message to him? She wasn't supposed to speak to him directly. Hopefully, there would be a way of reaching out to him without raising suspicions.

By the time morning came along, she'd had little sleep.

Showered and with a towel around her body, she stared at the clothes in the large wardrobe.

All the items hanging in the closet were the ones Zain had purchased when he'd abducted her.

She hadn't been reunited with her clothes. When she'd gone missing, Kojo had sent her luggage back to Bagumi while he'd gone searching for her because he'd needed to travel light. He'd kept her phone, in case she'd tried to contact it and passport in case she'd needed it when he found her.

The clothes Zain had given her were classy and comfortable without the expense of her usual attires. They were similar to what Ruby Bagumi would have worn ten years ago, not what the princess she'd become would wear.

A huge smile spread on her face.

She pulled on the navy linen shift dress with the delicate embroidered leaf patterns that she had worn the first day in Boma. It was another way of keeping the connection with him alive.

Over the past three weeks, that outspoken, passionate woman who believed in fighting for justice and equality had been revived, thanks to Zain. She didn't want to go back to having to bite her tongue when she should speak her mind or bowing to etiquettes and protocols all the time.

Still, she had to keep a balance, as Professor Bassong had taught her many years ago. There was a time for diplomacy and a time to stare your opponents in the face, weapons at the ready.

Dressed, she went into the living room. The television screen on the far wall showed the WTA channel.

"Good morning, Your Highness," Latifah said as she got off the cream upholstered sofa with gold trim.

The woman wore skinny black jeans and a blue tunic paired with chunky boots with metal buckles. Her hair had a fringe and was cut into a bob that stopped at her nape. She had a badass vibe that looked different from the demure woman who had been pushing a laundry cart the day they had first met.

"Morning, Latifah." Isha suppressed a shiver as she headed to the dining area.

Kojo stood beside the table. "Good morning, My Princess. Breakfast awaits."

"Morning, Kojo." She eyed the covered dishes. "I don't think I'll eat anything just yet. I'm not keen to eat any food from the Doonas' kitchen."

She might have to go out to a restaurant later.

"This is not from the presidential kitchen." Latifah joined them.

"It's not?" Isha glanced up in confusion.

"I don't trust these people," Latifah said.

"Neither do I," Kojo added as he pulled out a cream-cushioned, high-back armchair with gilded feet. "So I went out and stocked the kitchen in the apartment yesterday. I cooked this morning."

"You did?" She lowered her body onto the seat at the end of the rectangular glass-topped table. "I thought I was assigned service staff to cook and clean the place."

Kojo walked her left side and pulled out another chair.

"Yes, there are domestic employees available." Latifah sat in the spot while her bodyguard came around and sat on the chair by her right. "But none of them are allowed to cook your food. I promised Prof that I'd keep you safe, and I won't let anyone poison you."

"Poison?" Isha coughed in shock. "Why would anyone want to poison me?"

"He believes you were poisoned before, a decade ago, and the person will try it again."

A fluttering rose in Isha's stomach, and she shook her head in confusion. "What are you talking about? I wasn't poisoned."

"May I speak freely?" Latifah said, hands braced on the table.

"Of course." She waved her hand for the woman to spill already.

"Prof thinks you may be carrying his baby."

Isha's face flamed at the intrusion into her private life. She tugged at the collar of the dress as she averted her gaze. "I'm not pregnant."

At least, it was too early to tell.

However, they hadn't used protection, and she didn't take any form of contraception. She hadn't needed one since she'd been sexually inactive for so long. The plan had been to hopefully get pregnant soon after her wedding to Kweku.

She hadn't counted on reuniting with Zain and falling in love again.

And making another baby.

"He doesn't want to take any chances. He believes you were poisoned before. That's why you lost the baby."

Goodness!

She covered her face with both hands and slumped in the chair.

Knowing everything about Kweku's previous actions, poisoning her wasn't far-fetched.

She scrambled her brain, trying to remember events from so long ago.

When she'd discovered she'd been pregnant, her relationship with the professor had already ended. She'd been alone and desperate. She'd hidden the growing bump with baggy clothing. Amara had teased her once about the amount of food she consumed.

Then, she'd confessed and had made Amara promise not to tell anyone.

Kweku had come to see her once that autumn. He'd been in London on a brief visit and had stopped by with takeaway pizza and drinks. That night, she'd fallen ill.

"Oh, my goodness! He poisoned me! That freaking sonofabitch poisoned me." She shot off the chair and paced to the living room.

"He did?"

"Who did?"

Both Kojo and Latifah spoke at the same time and joined her.

"Who else? The Doona bastard. I'm going to kill him. I'm going to freaking kill him."

She'd had enough of being manipulated by Kweku. She turned to the two of them. "Are you armed?"

"Yes." Worry lines etched Kojo's forehead as he patted his chest, indicating the gun tucked in a shoulder strap under his jacket.

"So am I." Latifah lifted her right leg and slid a fearsome dagger with a jagged edge from the sheath in her boot. "What do you have in mind?"

"This nonsense ends today. Get my phone—"

The object on the coffee table vibrated, cutting her off.

"It is Prince Zik." Kojo handed the phone over.

She grabbed it and spoke without preamble. "Zik, I'm so glad you called."

"Hey. Are you alright?" He sounded concerned.

"Yes, I will be. Just tell me you have what I'm waiting for, please."

"Yes. The team got back yesterday, and I met with them last night. I couldn't believe what I saw in those videos. It was horrible. I'm getting ready to fly to Wanai today."

"I told you. I freaking told you." Isha's hands and body trembled at the relief. She didn't have to stay here any second longer. But she had one more thing to do first. "I need you to stay on the line and if possible record the audio. Can you do that?"

"Sure. I'll stay on the line," he said.

"Great." She handed the phone to Kojo. "Make sure the line stays connected. Come on."

Latifah held the door, and she walked out, her heels clicking on the marble tiles. She approached the uniformed guard outside Kweku's reception room.

"Good morning, Your Highness," he said. "Mr. Kweku is in a meeting."

She kept her face devoid of expression. "I'm expected at the meeting."

"Oh." He hesitated, shifting from one foot to the other.

"Go in and announce my presence," she said in a powerful voice.

He swallowed. "Yes, Your Highness."

He tapped on the door and opened it. "Excuse me, Sir. Princess Isha is here."

"Tell her to come back later," a female voice called out.

"Kojo, please open the door." Isha stood aside.

Taller Kojo reached above the guard's head and shoved the panel, startling him.

"What are you doing?" the man asked in a shocked voice, blocking the entrance.

"Stand aside for Her Highness, Princess Isha of the Kingdom of Bagumi," Kojo ordered in a domineering tone which made Isha smile briefly.

Head high, chin up, she sashayed into the reception room as the occupants—Kweku and his two sisters—turned in her direction.

Kweku stood from his sofa backing the far wall. "Isha, dear, is there a problem?"

He had a charming smile that hid an evil soul.

Isha's fingers tingled with the urge to slap the smirk off his face.

His older sister, Joanna, stood and approached her, eyes gleaming with insolence. "This is a private meeting, and you have not been invited."

The woman had always been jealous of Isha and had been known to make snide remarks. She'd overheard her once refer to Isha as 'the fat princess' to her friends at a party. Isha had brushed it off at the time, knowing Joanna wished her father was a king instead of a dictator. The sophisticated and composed Princess Isha Saene wouldn't stoop low to exchange words with a commoner.

Now, that princess was nowhere in sight as Isha swung her right arm and smacked Joanna across the left cheek. "Sit your bony ass down, bitch."

The woman jerked back, speechless and wide-eyed, holding her face.

Marianna, her younger sister, gasped, hand covering her mouth.

"Joanna, are you okay?" Kweku rushed to his sister. "Isha, why did you hit her?"

"Why shouldn't I? She is rude, antagonistic, arrogant, envious, evil, immoral?" She counted off on her fingers. "Should I go on? Someone should have taken a belt to her ass a long time ago."

"That's no reason to hit my sister," he bit out angrily, his arm around his sister.

"Says the murderer." She clicked her tongue.

"What did you call me?" Kweku narrowed his eyes and straightened.

"I called you a murderer because that's what you are." She glared at him.

Kojo stepped forward, standing beside her in case Kweku tried anything, his hands loosened by his side. Latifah stood by the closed door in an alert stance.

"She's gone mad," Joanna shouted.

"Says the woman who has been having sex with her sister's husband," Isha commented.

"What?" Marianna glanced from Isha to Joanna. "Is that true?"

Joanna looked away, lips tight.

"Oh. It's very true. I have video and audio recordings of both of them." Isha looked at her fingers nails as if disinterested in the conversation.

"You bitch!" Marianna screamed and rushed at Joanna.

Kweku intercepted her and held them apart. "Calm down and behave yourself, both of you."

Marianna returned to her chair, still glowering at her sister.

Kweku turned his glare on Isha. "What the hell is the matter with you?"

"Oh, come on. I'm the first daughter of a king. One of the first things I learned about power is to 'keep my friends close and my enemies even closer.' Did you really think I would marry into your family without leverage? I had all of you investigated. For example, my darling Kweku, you have several mistresses. I know about each one of them, where they live, how much you spend on their allowances." She made air quotes with her fingers.

Kweku jerked backwards as if she'd slapped him. His mouth opened, but no words came out.

"And you, Marianna. You seem to be the only innocent person in this family. I pity you for being part of such a corrupt family. On a serious note, if you need a good divorce lawyer, call me. I have several friends that can help you take your cheating husband to the cleaners."

"That's enough." Kweku seemed to have found his voice and stomped in her direction. "You are my fiancée, for fuck's sake. Why are you doing this?"

Isha gulped in air, straightened her shoulders. "I welcomed you into my home once. Ten years ago, you came with Zawadi to visit me in London. You poisoned me."

His eyes went wide, and he jerked back.

"What did you give me?" she asked in a hard voice.

"Look. It wasn't like that. I wasn't trying to poison you."

"So, what was it like?"

He stood still, his gaze bounced around the room. "I came to London to see you. You were always meant to be mine right from when Zawadi and I became friends. But then, we came to visit you in London, and I found out you were pregnant."

"How did you know? I never told you. Hardly even spoke to you back then. The only reason you knew was because you hacked into Zain's account and saw the email I sent him." she asked.

He lifted his shoulders in a blasé shrug. "I had enough girlfriends get pregnant to know the early signs. And you showed them. There was no way I was going to let you have another man's child when you were supposed to be mine. So I gave you a drug to induce a miscarriage. It wasn't meant to kill you."

Isha's blood ran cold, and she sucked in a sharp breath. "You killed my baby instead."

"I did you a favour."

She balled her fists. "You did me a favour? You're an arrogant bastard. You committed murder."

"That's nonsense."

"We'll see if it's nonsense when you're arrested."

His laughter echoed off the baroque wallpapers. "I'm the son of the head of state and the next president of Wanai. No one can arrest me."

Her hands curled into balls, and she had to quash the urge to smash them into his pompous face.

He'd killed her unborn baby and had destroyed her relationship with Zain many years ago, and showed no ounce of remorse.

If she had a gun, she would've shot him. Death was perhaps too simple a punishment for him. However, she would get justice one way or the other.

"You're not president yet." She loaded her words with as much menace as she could.

"Are you threatening me?"

"You bet I am. Even if I can't get you for murdering my baby, you will be indicted for murdering thousands of Wanai civilians."

"What ridiculousness? *I* am going to be your husband."

Isha stepped forward. "You and your father are perpetrating genocide. You are killing your own citizens."

"You can't prove anything."

"You think you're untouchable, son of the president and all." Her words dripped with disdain. "You are swine."

She flicked her hand up and down at him.

"Don't you dare talk to me like that!" He balled his hands.

"If you want respect, then be a man. Admit what you have done, and I will give you all the respect you deserve."

She pushed him, knowing how much he wanted the respect that came with the Saene name. And by marrying her, the honour would be transferred to him.

"You bet I deserve respect. But I will admit nothing."

"You really are a swine not worth my time. I'm out of here." She turned to leave.

"You're not going anywhere. You are not allowed out of the palace."

She swivelled to face him. "I'm not allowed out of the palace? Am I a prisoner?"

"We made a deal. You agreed to stay in the palace until our wedding rites are completed."

"Do you know how pathetic and desperate you sound?" She shook her head in pity. "I'm never going to marry you."

"No. No. You are not backing out of it. You are going to be my wife, and you are not to leave this palace without my permission."

"Are you sure about that?" She kept her hands on her hips.

"Of course, I'm sure."

"So you bring an enemy into the presidential palace," she said in a calm voice, and his eyes widened. "Oh, yes, I am your enemy. An enemy of the entire Doona family."

Marianna gasped. "Kweku?"

"She's bluffing," he replied.

"Am I? Do you want to bet your life on it? I just found out you killed my baby. I'm distraught. Joanna already mentioned that I was mad. Can you predict what I will do?" She took a step forward. "You want to keep me here? Go ahead. But I will burn this freaking building down first before I marry you, and I'll make sure you're in it when it burns."

"You wouldn't."

"Try me and see. I'm ready to die for the people I love. Can you say the same, Kweku?"

The three siblings had stunned expression as she swivelled and walked out of the reception room, head high.

CHAPTER TWENTY-SEVEN

"PLEASE state your name."

"Princess Isha Saene."

A blue LED flashed on the video camera mounted on a tripod in the corner.

A man sat in an armchair across from her, his expression eager and inquisitive. He was from the Office of the Prosecutor at the International Criminal Court and conducting preliminary examinations based on the report she had sent to them.

Zik had made sure the process was expedited once the evidence had been collected. He'd even paid for the team from the ICC to travel to Bagumi for this session at the earliest opportunity.

The man from the ICC rattled off the procedure for the interview and what would happen afterwards during the investigations.

His job was to determine if there was sufficient evidence of heinous crimes and if those crimes fell under the jurisdiction of the ICC. He also had to decide whether opening an investigation would deliver justice for the victims.

"Please explain why you contacted the ICC."

"I have evidence of crimes against humanity being perpetrated by the government of Wanai."

She went ahead to explain what she had witnessed during her visits through Ganuri.

Projecting outward calm, she kept her voice emotionless. Inside, her turmoil rolled and crashed.

If the man felt disturbed by her descriptions of events, he didn't show it aside from the occasional adjustment of his tie.

His questions kept coming, designed to delve and discover the truth. He'd probably interviewed many victims of atrocities so her account must appear ordinary since she wouldn't be classified as a victim.

Recounting her time in Ganuri reminded her of Zain. Not that she hadn't thought about him every day for the past week.

All the emotions bubbled inside as she remembered the passion in his voice when he'd spoken about the future. He wanted a better life for his people and the whole of Wanai. And in those precious private moments they'd had together, his love and desire for her had been evident in his touch and words, too.

By the time the interview ended and the man left promising to be in touch, her hands trembled, left raw with emotions.

She'd returned to Bagumi with her brother a few days ago. Kweku had had little choice but to let her go after their confrontation. She'd wanted to begin the ICC process and hopefully take the ICC investigator back to Ganuri when she returned.

For that, she'd needed to gain political support from her father and Zawadi as they were close to the Doonas.

In the quiet of her apartment, she yearned for Zain. She missed him, his home.

Her gaze swept the living area. Hopefully, he'd get the chance to visit Bagumi and see where she lived soon. She would introduce him to her parents like she should have done ten years ago.

So many things for them to experience in the future.

She should call him. But due to the problems with phone lines in Ganuri, the only stable connection was the satellite phone. And he preferred they spoke in the evenings when he didn't have other distractions.

A tap on her bedroom door jarred her out of her reverie.

"Who is it?" she called out.

Kojo popped his head in. "Your Highness, you have a guest."

"A guest? Did I miss something on my schedule? I have a meeting with Papa and Zawadi in a few minutes."

She crossed the threshold and saw Zik. "It's you. I thought we were meeting later."

He kissed her cheek. "Hey, sis. I have a surprise for you."

Movement at the periphery of her vision made her turn. A man stood from the sofa, his back to her.

Her heart thumped hard as she recognised the tall, broad-shouldered man.

"Zain." She hurried across the living room as he turned, his lips curled in the most glorious grin.

They collided, arms wrapped around each other, clinging tight.

"I can't believe you're here." She looked up at him with misty eyes.

He grinned at her, kissing her forehead. "If the mountain won't go to Mohammed, then Mohammed must go to the mountain. I had to see you for myself and know you're okay after your encounter with the Doonas."

"I'm fine. Everything is fine. How did you get here?" She couldn't believe he'd been allowed through the palace security without clearance.

"Your brother smuggled me in." He glanced in Zik's direction.

She swivelled to look at her sibling. "You did?"

His brother had a smirk on his face. "I figured since you're presenting your case to be with him to the judge and jury today, the accused should be there."

She laughed at his reference to their parents as 'judge and jury.' Still, he was correct. She would have to defend Zain before her family.

"And you didn't tell me?" She walked over and kissed him on the cheek. "Thank you."

"I wanted to surprise you."

"You are such a romantic."

"Don't tell that to anyone." He winked. "I have a player reputation to maintain."

"You are so incorrigible." She giggled.

"Thanks again for your help," Zain said as they shook hands.

"Well, the deal is that you take care of my sister. Plus I might need somewhere to escape to on the days I get fed up with being a prince. And you both now owe me."

"We are going to name our first born son after you as thank you," she said, teasing him in return.

"Hell, no. There's only one Azikiwe in this family."

They all laughed.

"Anyway, I better leave you two to get reacquainted." He headed towards the exit and glanced at his watch. "I'll keep the rest of them entertained. You have thirty minutes."

"Oh, you!" She picked up a cushion and tossed it.

It hit the closed door as his chuckles rang in the air.

Breathless, she turned to Zain who watched with the dark expression that sent a sizzle down her spine.

"So this is what a palace looks like," he teased, eyes gleaming with mischief.

She placed her hands akimbo. "Did you come here to admire the architecture?"

He pulled something out of the leather bag beside the sofa, hid it behind his back, and stalked towards her. "I came to rescue the princess from the tower."

Black leather cuffs linked by a metal chain dangled from his raised hand.

"Oh." Her pulse skyrocketed, and her knees weakened. She swallowed. "We can't."

She couldn't seem to work her tongue and backed off towards the bedroom.

She wanted him so much. To have sex in the palace was against all protocol. He shouldn't be here without a chaperone.

She glanced around. Kojo and Latifah had disappeared, conveniently.

"What can't we do?" He continued his approach.

"We can't have sex," she said in almost a whisper as if the walls were listening.

"So you don't want me to bind your hands to that four-poster bed, spread your thighs, and eat your pussy until you come all over my face."

"Zain," she cried out as her clit throbbed and her insides contracted. Her knickers dampened.

"Oh, well." He moved as if returning to the living room.

She didn't let him take a step before she jumped on him.

Their frenzied kisses only broke apart so they could remove each other's clothing. Soon, they were on the bed, and he fulfilled his promise, using his tongue and teeth and hands to send her to ecstasy. Then, he flipped her over, tugged her to her knees, and rode her to their completion.

By the time they'd showered, changed—Zain in a navy suit, white shirt, and black brogues, her in a beige, silk knee-length dress and strappy high-heeled sandals—and left her apartment together to walk down the vaulted corridors leading to her parents' quarters, forty minutes had passed.

Outside her father's reception room, she sent one of the guards in with a message for Zik.

Her brother came out shortly. "You're just in time. They just finished watching the video from the Ganuri investigators. Papa is quizzing Zawadi about his friend Kweku. Are you ready?"

"Oh, God." Isha's heart thumped hard in her chest, and her body trembled. More than anything else in the world, she wanted her parents to approve of Zain.

"We'll be alright." Zain squeezed her hand.

She nodded and clutched the ruby pendant dangling from her neck. She wished it was a lucky charm and would influence the proceeding. "Yes, we will."

The guard held the door.

She walked in first, still holding onto Zain.

Antique paintings, metal and wooden sculptures documenting the history of Bagumi lined the white walls. A large hand-woven rug covered the aisle from the door to the platform with three hand-carved heavy wooden chairs. The one in the middle had gemstones embedded in it to signify the status of the grey-haired man who sat in its regal glory.

His flowing robe had colourful patterns representing the colours of the gems extracted from the Bagumian mines.

The consorts sat on either of him—to the right Queen Zulekha, the first wife, and on the left Queen Sapphire, her mother. Her brother Zawadi stood to the side and one step down. They spoke in low voices.

Halfway to the dais, she halted and curtseyed. Zain bowed.

"Long live King Ibrahim and The Royal House of Saene," they said together.

She had briefed Zain on the protocol for his first meeting with her father. She didn't want anything to go wrong.

Her parents looked in their direction.

"Isha, is that you?" her father's voice boomed.

"Yes, Papa." She stepped up to the dais and knelt before her father.

He leaned forward and pulled her up into a hug. "I haven't seen you in a long while. How have you been?"

"I'm well, Papa." She turned her attention to Queen Zulekha as she curtseyed. "Mama, you're looking fantastic."

They referred to the first queen as 'Mama' because of her seniority while Isha's birth mother was 'Mum.'

The older woman beamed a smile and patted her shoulders. "Thank you. You've learnt how to sweet-talk from Zik?"

She smiled coyly. She needed to keep all of them sweet because of the announcement she was about to make.

Then, she approached her mother, who gave her a tight hug and whispered in her ear, "I'm glad that you are safe and well."

"Thank you, Mum," she said in a choked voice and faced her oldest brother. "Hello, Zawadi."

"I was not aware that you had a guest." Her sibling's voice was cold, his expression grim as he stared at Zain.

"Yes. I'd like to present Professor Zain Bassong."

Zain came forward and prostrated. "Your Majesty, I am humbled to be in your presence."

Isha gasped. She had told him to bow, which was a reasonable enough deference.

However, a full prostrate was the ultimate show of submission to her father's authority. No one could fault it.

"Rise, Professor," the king said. "Your name sounds familiar. Have we met?"

"Papa," Isha said before Zain could respond. "He is from Ganuri. I believe you have just watched the video of the atrocities committed against his people."

She needed to keep Kweku's crimes at the top of their minds.

"Oh, yes," Queen Sapphire said. "Those were horrible scenes. Imagine all those women and children in those camps. We must do something about it."

"We are, Mum," Isha said. "We've submitted a case file to the International Criminal Courts who have started their investigations."

"Does Kweku know about this?" Zawadi asked, still glaring at Zain.

"Yes, he does. He and his father are the accused."

"You can't be serious. The only person guilty of a crime is the terrorist you brought into this palace." Zawadi pointed at Zain. "Papa, that man is the lecturer Isha had an affair with when she was in London. He is also the leader of the separatist group fighting to split from Wanai."

"No, it's not true. He's not a terrorist." Isha stepped down to stand beside Zain. Her stomach churned, and her chest tightened.

He squeezed her trembling hand before bowing again. "Your Majesty, it is true that I met your daughter when she was in London. While I didn't know at the time that she was a princess, I did the wrong thing by not following the appropriate channels to seek your approval. For that, I am truly sorry and seek your forgiveness. I am here now because I love your daughter and wish to marry her with your approval."

"That may be so, young man," the king said. "But no terrorist is going to marry my daughter."

"Your Majesty, I swear to you on my life that I have never committed any of the crimes that Doona accuses me of. Prince Azikiwe sent spies into Ganuri to document the events. If he found any evidence of members of my group persecuting the citizens, I'm sure he would have presented them to you today."

"That's true, Papa." Zik stood on the other side of Zain. "The intelligence officers that went into Ganuri found no evidence of crimes committed by the MLG. Instead, the group have provided safe zones and shelter for the people who have been attacked. There is genocide going on, and all fingers point to Doona, especially Kweku who has been arresting and torturing the people campaigning for independence."

"That's the other thing," her father said, giving Zain an inscrutable look. "I'm not pleased about this fight for independence. If Wanai breaks up, it will destabilise the region."

"Your Majesty, my people are willing to live in Wanai as long as they can live peacefully without persecution. That's not going to happen while President Doona or members of his cabal are in power."

"Hmmm," the king murmured as if musing over the words.

"Papa, are you even considering this? Kweku wouldn't do those things," Zawadi said.

"Brother, you have to give it up. I heard him on the phone bragging about poisoning Isha years ago."

"No way!" Queen Sapphire exclaimed.

"It's true, Mama," Isha said. "He confessed it a few days ago."

"You are definitely not going to marry him," her mother said.

"I know, Mama. The wedding is off."

The room went silent.

After long seconds, the king spoke. "Young man, I know my daughter will not bring you here unless she loved you. All my children are unique and brilliant. Isha is a woman with the heart of a lioness. And Zawadi knows that I love him. However, if Isha had been male, I would have named her as my heir."

Both queens gasped.

According to Bagumian noble tradition, the throne was passed to the firstborn son unless he was deemed unsuitable for a variety of reasons. If Isha were male, she would be third in line after Zawadi and Zik.

Warmth spread across Isha's chest. She hadn't heard such praise from her father since she was a small child. "Thank you, Papa."

The king waved her off with a smile. "I say this not as a slight on Zawadi or any of my sons because each one of them will make a good king. However, Isha is the only one not afraid to challenge my authority. As a teenager, she gave up the privileges that came with being a royal princess, something none of her siblings has attempted. She has enough courage to follow her convictions, which is why she will still go with you whether I approve or not. And she is likely to lead a rebellion to topple our kingdom and status quo. So perhaps she should go to Wanai, after all, and teach your citizens the responsibility of power."

Her father laughed, and everyone else joined in.

"Papa!"

Isha's cheeks heated as she smiled shyly. Her father's teasing proved he was in good spirits. Her heart raced in anticipation as she glanced at the man standing beside her. Finally, it seemed she would have all the things she desired.

Zain had a grin on his face and squeezed her hand again. "Your Majesty, I believe your daughter will make a great president. I would certainly vote for her."

Her father nodded. "On a serious note, I want my daughter's happiness, and it seems she finds it in you. So this time, you will do it properly. No more sneaking around. We are already planning for a wedding. The groom might be different, but there's going to be a wedding."

Epilogue

THE road from dictatorship to democracy was not an easy one for Wanai.

In the early hours of one morning in July Twenty-Eighteen, while Isha and Zain were on their honeymoon in The Gambia, news broke on the radio about a coup d'état.

The military led by Lieutenant General Jeremiah Kamto had overthrown the thirty-five-year government of President Doona.

In his speech, General Kamto said the military had had to act following the continued civil unrest and the mass killings of civilians, and he promised a transition to multi-party democracy within the twelve months. He was also in discussions with the International Criminal Court about handing over named members of the Doona family while they were under house arrest.

The next week, Isha and Zain returned to Boma and were greeted by cheering crowds and journalists and announced that they had set up the Viva Party. Within months, they were touring around the country on the campaign trail, and Isha always gave the introduction speech and concluded with:

"My name is Princess Isha Saene-Bassong, and my husband is running for the president of the Republic of Wanai."

Thank you for reading His Captive Princess.

If you enjoyed this story, remember to leave a review at the site of purchase.

Also visit Kiru Taye's website at www.kirutaye.com for more book news.

OTHER BOOKS BY LOVE AFRICA PRESS

Healing His Medic by Nana Prah

Queer and Sexy Collection Volume 1

His Defiant Princess by Nana Prah

His Inherited Princess by Empi Baryeh

Be My Valentine Anthology by various authors

Ere's Secret & 223 Bonny Street by Firi Kamson

Love at First Sound by Amaka Azie

Dawsk by Erhu Kome Yellow

CONNECT WITH US

Facebook.com/LoveAfricaPress

Twitter.com/LoveAfricaPress

Instagram.com/LoveAfricaPress

www.loveafricapress.com